5/18

AVENGERS K #2
THE ADVENT OF ULTRON

Following the death of their parents, twins Pietro and Wanda Maximoff think they've found a new place to call home. But when their mutant powers are exposed, they're branded demons-saved only by the arrival of Magneto, the Master of Magnetism! Now calling themselves Quicksilver and the Scarlet Witch, the twins join Magneto's war for mutantkind. But with tensions building in their new team, Quicksilver makes a shocking discovery!

JIM ZUB
SCRIPT

WOO BIN CHOI WITH **JAE SUNG LEE**
ART

MIN JU LEE
ART

JAE WOONG LEE
COLORS

VC'S CORY PETIT
LETTERS

WOO BIN CHOI WITH **JAE SUNG LEE, MIN JU LEE** & **JAE WOONG LEE**
COVER ART

AVENGERS VS. ULTRON is adapted from AVENGERS ORIGINS: SCARLET WITCH & QUICKSILVER #1, AVENGERS ORIGINS: ANT-MAN & THE WASP #1, and AVENGERS (1963) #57.
Adaptations written by SI YEON PARK and translated by JI EUN PARK

AVENGERS created by STAN LEE and JACK KIRBY

Original comics written by SEAN McKEEVER, ROBERTO AGUIRRE-SACASA, and ROY THOMAS; and illustrated by MIRCO PIERFEDERICI, STEPHANIE HANS, and JOHN BUSCEMA

Editor SARAH BRUNSTAD
Manager, Licensed Publishing JEFF REINGOLD
VP, Brand Management & Development, Asia C.B. CEBULSKI
VP, Production & Special Projects JEFF YOUNGQUIST
SVP Print, Sales & Marketing DAVID GABRIEL
Associate Manager, Digital Assets JOE HOCHSTEIN
Associate Managing Editor ALEX STARBUCK
Senior Editor, Special Projects JENNIFER GRÜNWALD
Editor, Special Projects MARK D. BEAZLEY
Book Designer ADAM DEL RE

Editor In Chief AXEL ALONSO
Chief Creative Officer JOE QUESADA
President DAN BUCKLEY
Executive Producer ALAN FINE

ABDO
Spotlight

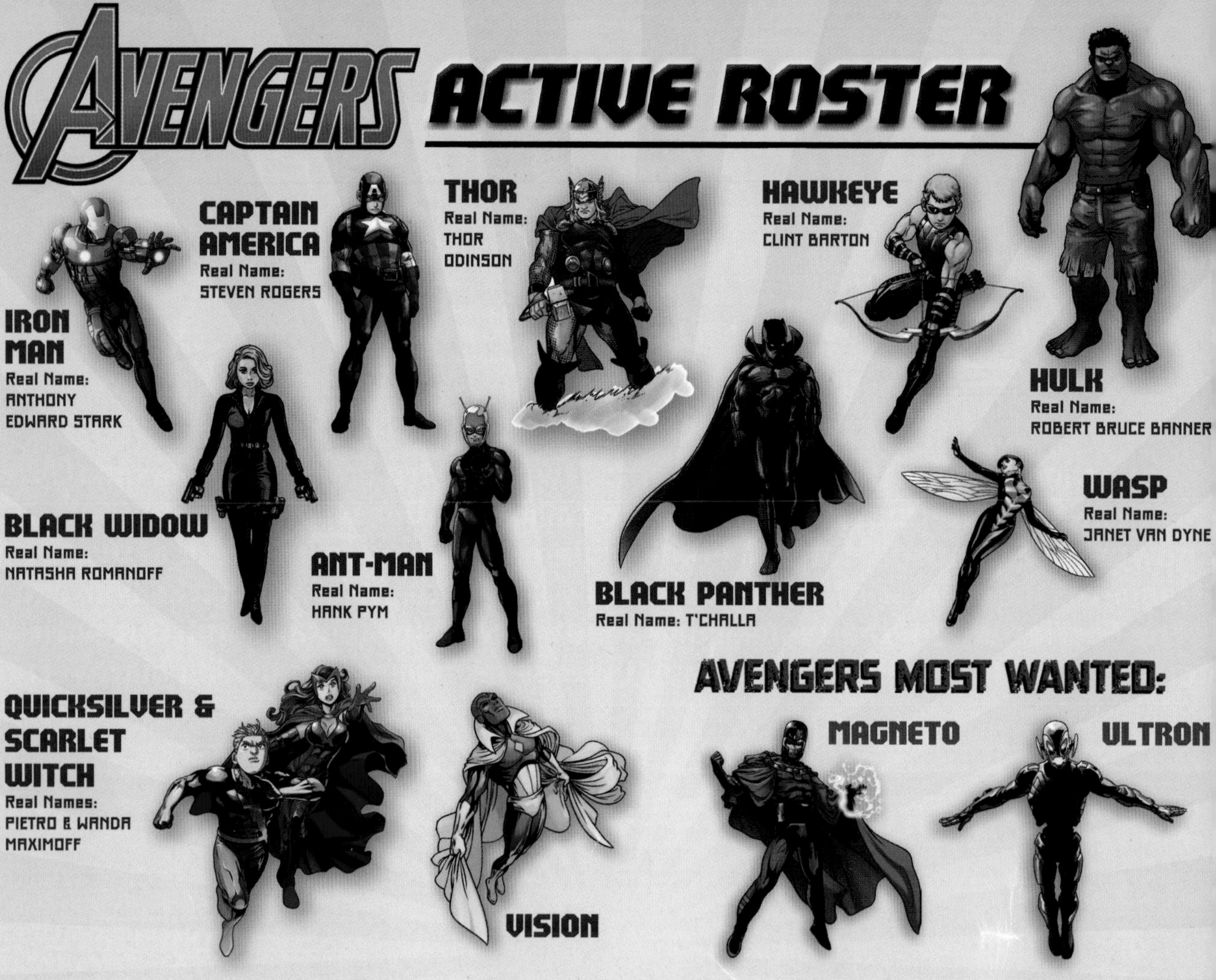
AVENGERS
ACTIVE ROSTER
IRON MAN
Real Name:
ANTHONY EDWARD STARK
CAPTAIN AMERICA
Real Name:
STEVEN ROGERS
THOR
Real Name:
THOR ODINSON
HAWKEYE
Real Name:
CLINT BARTON
HULK
Real Name:
ROBERT BRUCE BANNER
BLACK WIDOW
Real Name:
NATASHA ROMANOFF
ANT-MAN
Real Name:
HANK PYM
BLACK PANTHER
Real Name: T'CHALLA
WASP
Real Name:
JANET VAN DYNE
QUICKSILVER & SCARLET WITCH
Real Names:
PIETRO & WANDA MAXIMOFF
VISION
AVENGERS MOST WANTED:
MAGNETO
ULTRON

ABDOPUBLISHING.COM

Reinforced library bound edition published in 2018 by Spotlight, a division of ABDO, PO Box 398166, Minneapolis, Minnesota 55439.
Spotlight produces high-quality reinforced library bound editions for schools and libraries. Published by agreement with Marvel Characters, Inc.
Printed in the United States of America, North Mankato, Minnesota.
042017 092017

marvelkids.com

THIS BOOK CONTAINS RECYCLED MATERIALS

PUBLISHER'S CATALOGING IN PUBLICATION DATA

Names: Zub, Jim, author. | Choi, Woo Bin ; Lee, Jae Sung ; Lee, Min Ju ; Lee, Jae Woong, illustrators.
Title: The advent of Ultron / writer: Jim Zub ; art: Woo Bin Choi ; Jae Sung Lee ; Min Ju Lee ; Jae Woong Lee.
Description: Reinforced library bound edition. | Minneapolis, Minnesota : Spotlight, 2018. | Series: Avengers K Set 2
Summary: Learn about the beginnings of your favorite Avengers, including Quicksilver and the Scarlet Witch's time with Magneto, how Ant-Man and the Wasp became a team, and the Vision's struggle to understand where he came from.
Identifiers: LCCN 2016961923 | ISBN 9781532140013 (v.1 ; lib. bdg.) | ISBN 9781532140020 (v.2 ; lib. bdg.) | ISBN 9781532140037 (v.3 ; lib. bdg.) | ISBN 9781532140044 (v.4 ; lib. bdg.) | ISBN 9781532140051 (v.5 ; lib. bdg.) | ISBN 9781532140068 (v.6 ; lib. bdg.)
Subjects: LCSH: Avengers (Fictitious characters)--Juvenile fiction. | Adventure and adventurers--Juvenile fiction. | Comic books, strips, etc.--Juvenile fiction. | Graphic novels--Juvenile fiction.
Classification: DDC 741.5--dc23
LC record available at https://lccn.loc.gov/2016961923

Spotlight

A Division of ABDO
abdopublishing.com

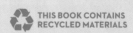

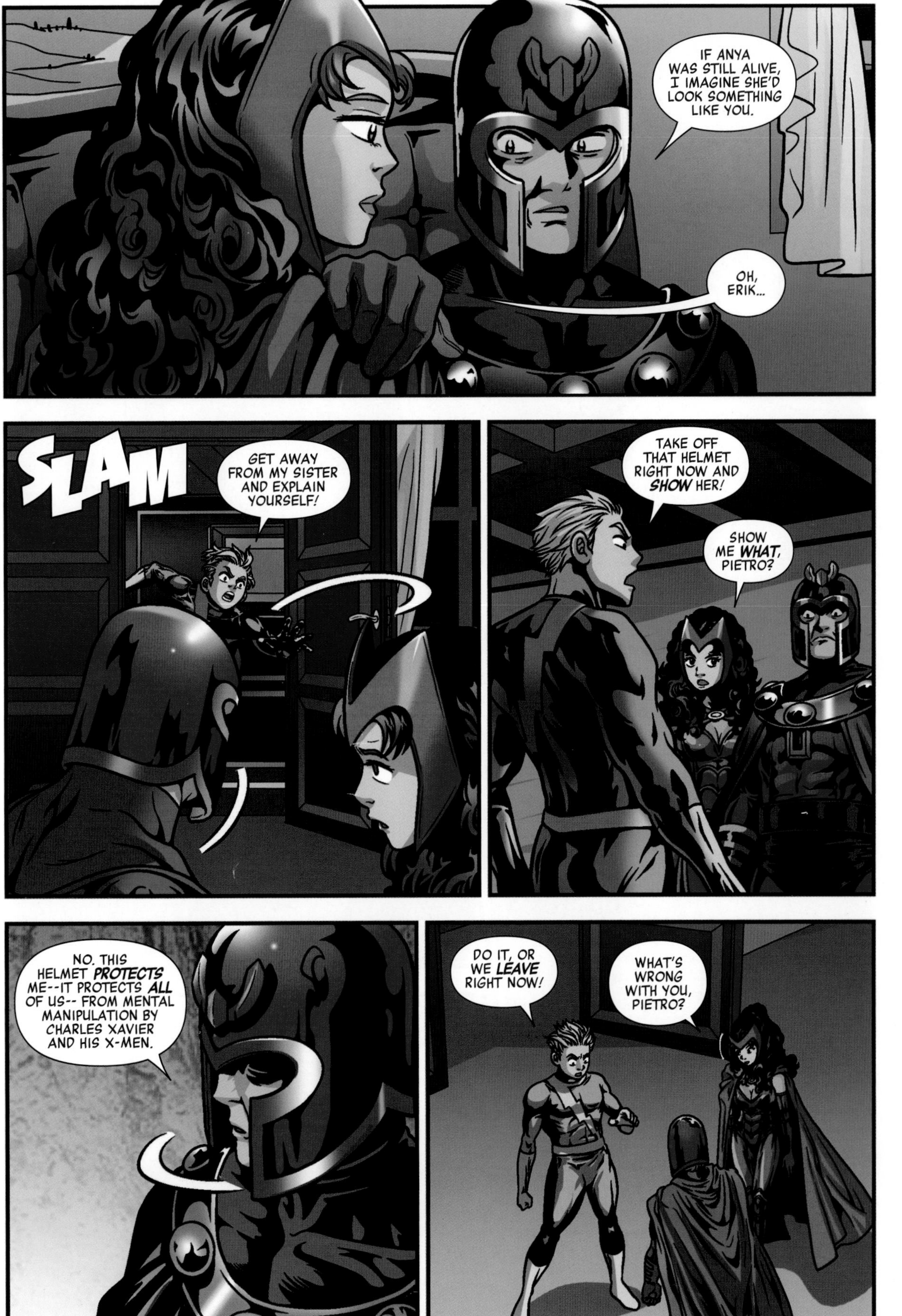
IF ANYA WAS STILL ALIVE, I IMAGINE SHE'D LOOK SOMETHING LIKE YOU.
OH, ERIK...
SLAM
GET AWAY FROM MY SISTER AND EXPLAIN YOURSELF!
TAKE OFF THAT HELMET RIGHT NOW AND SHOW HER!
SHOW ME WHAT, PIETRO?
NO. THIS HELMET PROTECTS ME--IT PROTECTS ALL OF US-- FROM MENTAL MANIPULATION BY CHARLES XAVIER AND HIS X-MEN.
DO IT, OR WE LEAVE RIGHT NOW!
WHAT'S WRONG WITH YOU, PIETRO?

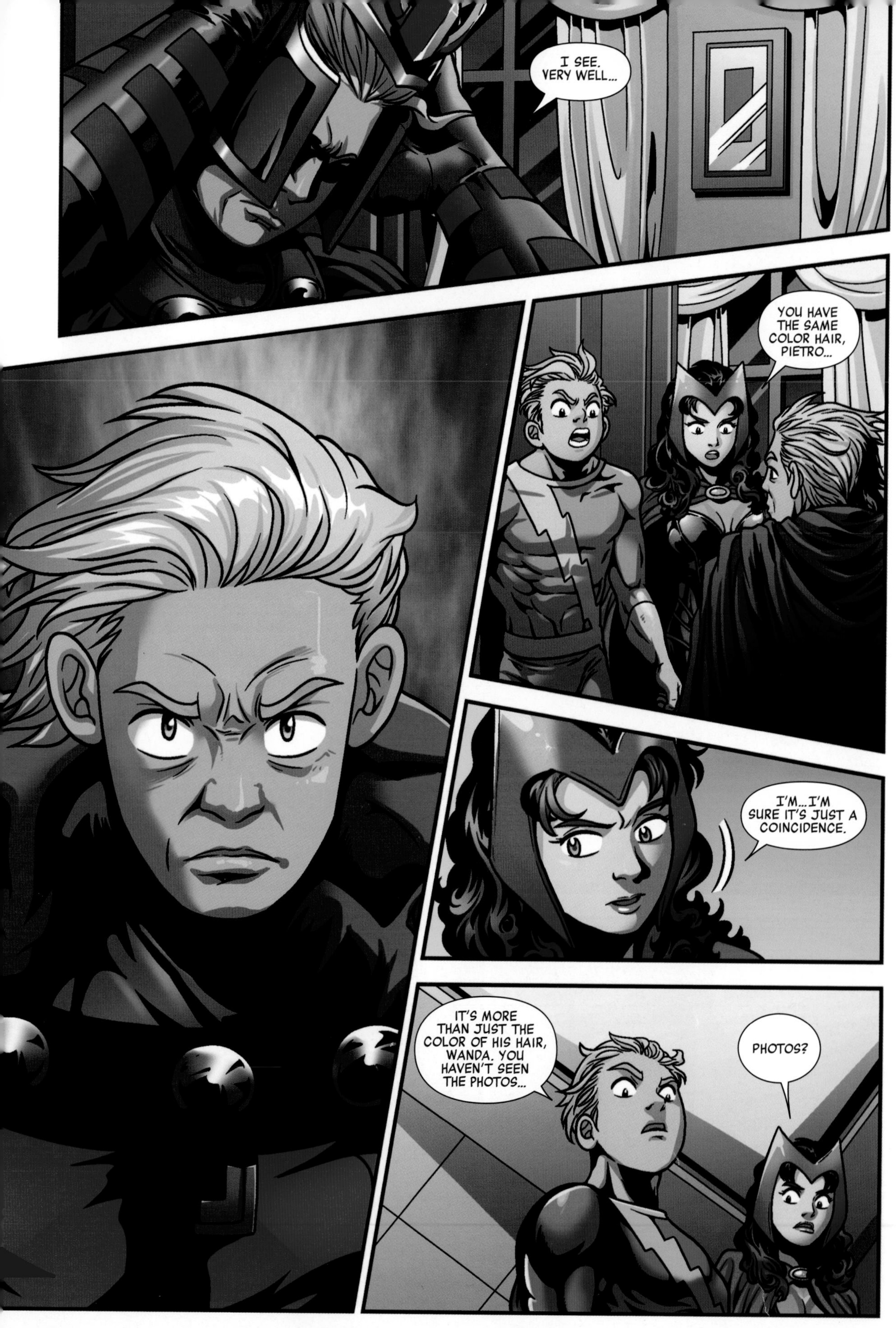
I SEE. VERY WELL...
YOU HAVE THE SAME COLOR HAIR, PIETRO...
I'M... I'M SURE IT'S JUST A COINCIDENCE.
IT'S MORE THAN JUST THE COLOR OF HIS HAIR, WANDA. YOU HAVEN'T SEEN THE PHOTOS...
PHOTOS?

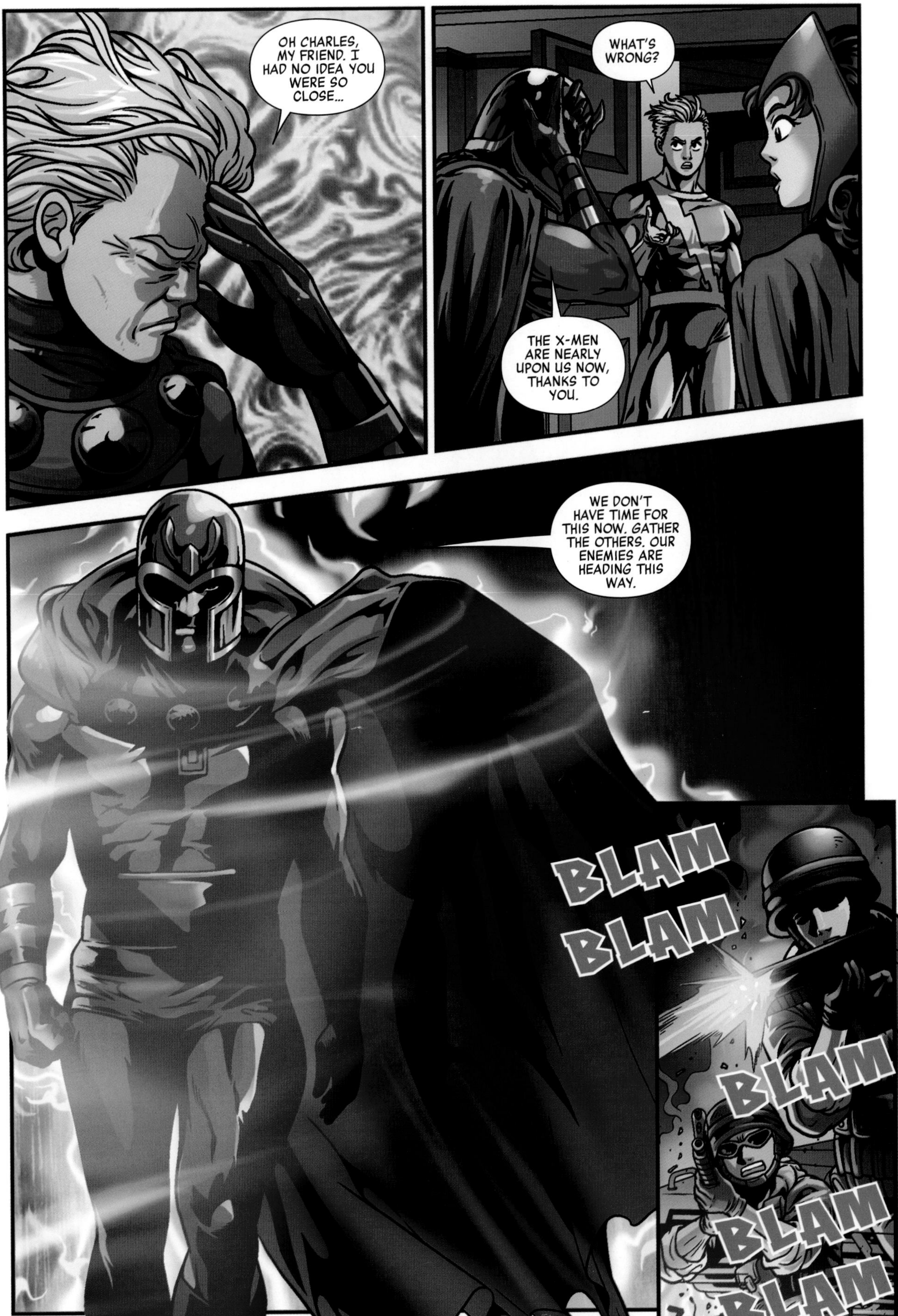
OH CHARLES, MY FRIEND. I HAD NO IDEA YOU WERE SO CLOSE...
WHAT'S WRONG?
THE X-MEN ARE NEARLY UPON US NOW, THANKS TO YOU.
WE DON'T HAVE TIME FOR THIS NOW. GATHER THE OTHERS. OUR ENEMIES ARE HEADING THIS WAY.
BLAM
BLAM
BLAM
BLAM
BLAM

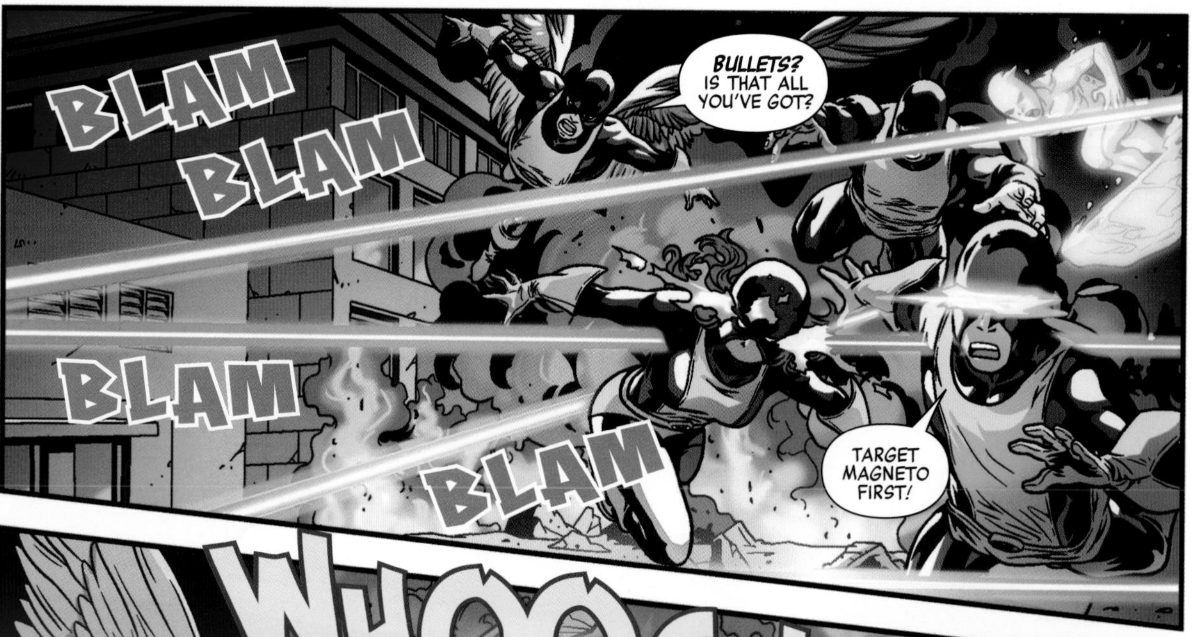
BLAM
BLAM
BULLETS? IS THAT ALL YOU'VE GOT?
BLAM
BLAM
TARGET MAGNETO FIRST!

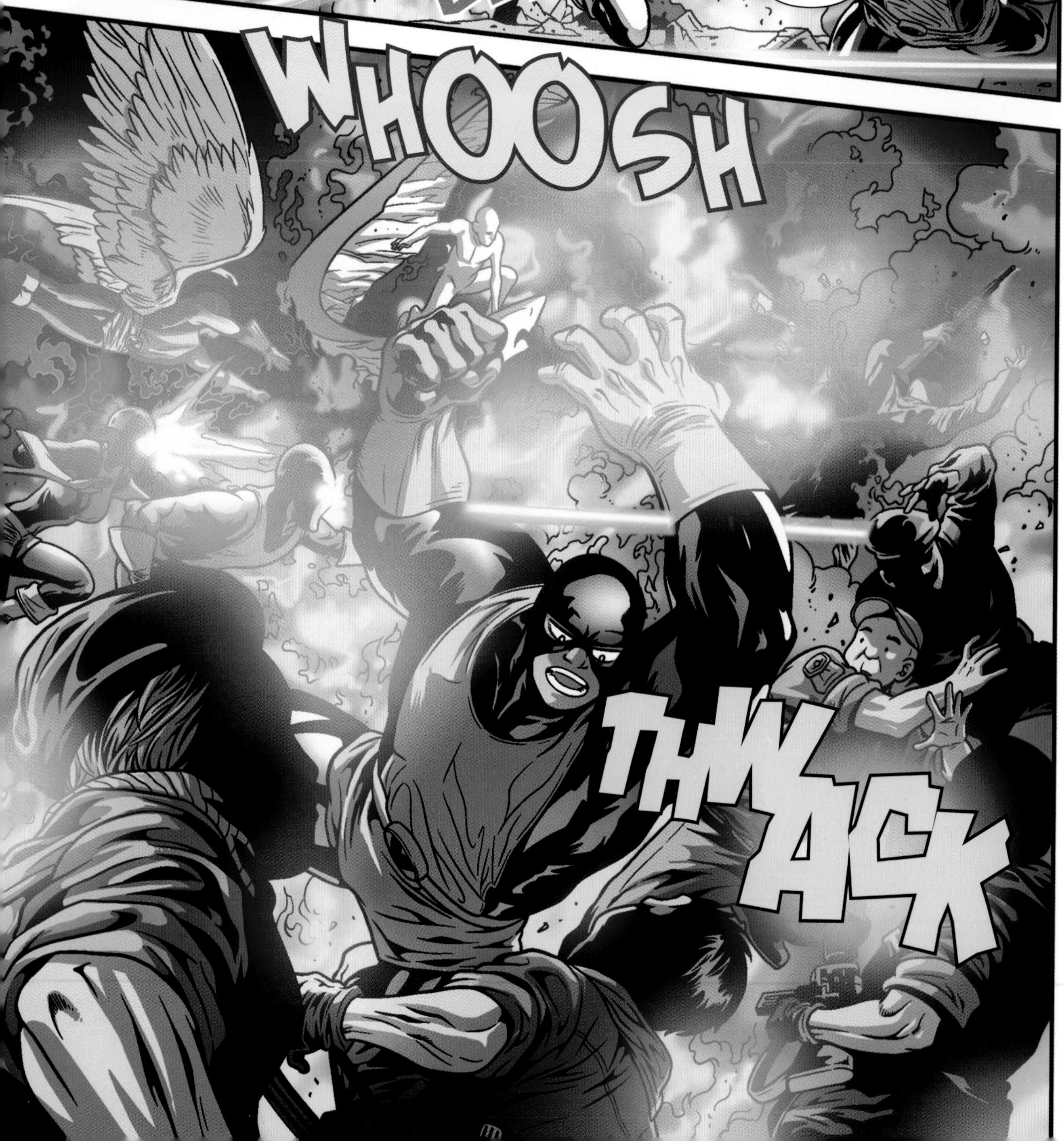
WHOOSH
THWACK

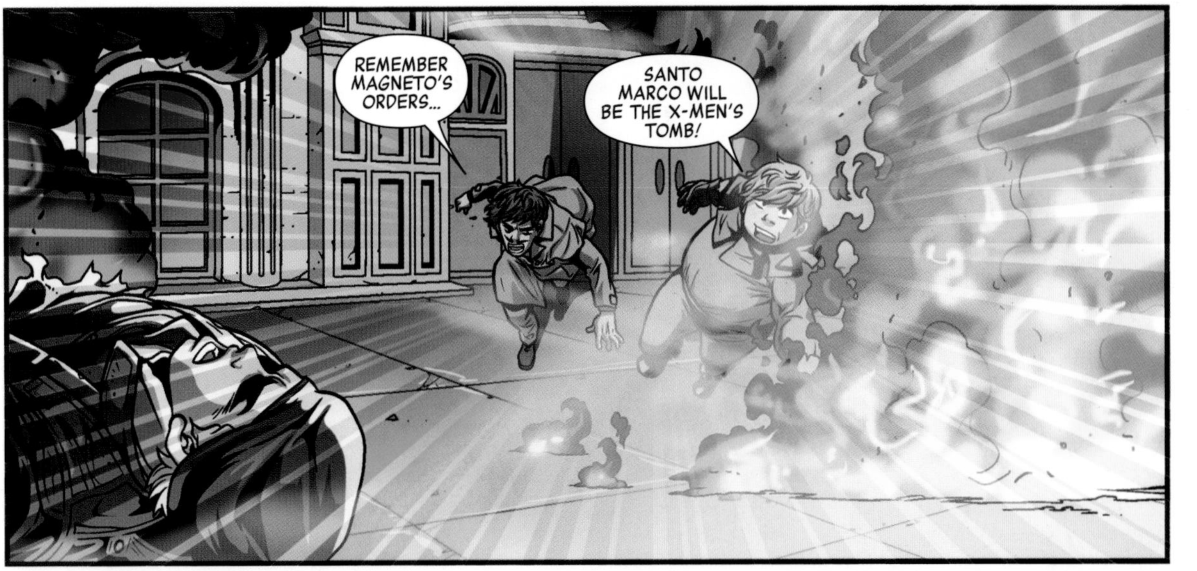
REMEMBER MAGNETO'S ORDERS...
SANTO MARCO WILL BE THE X-MEN'S TOMB!

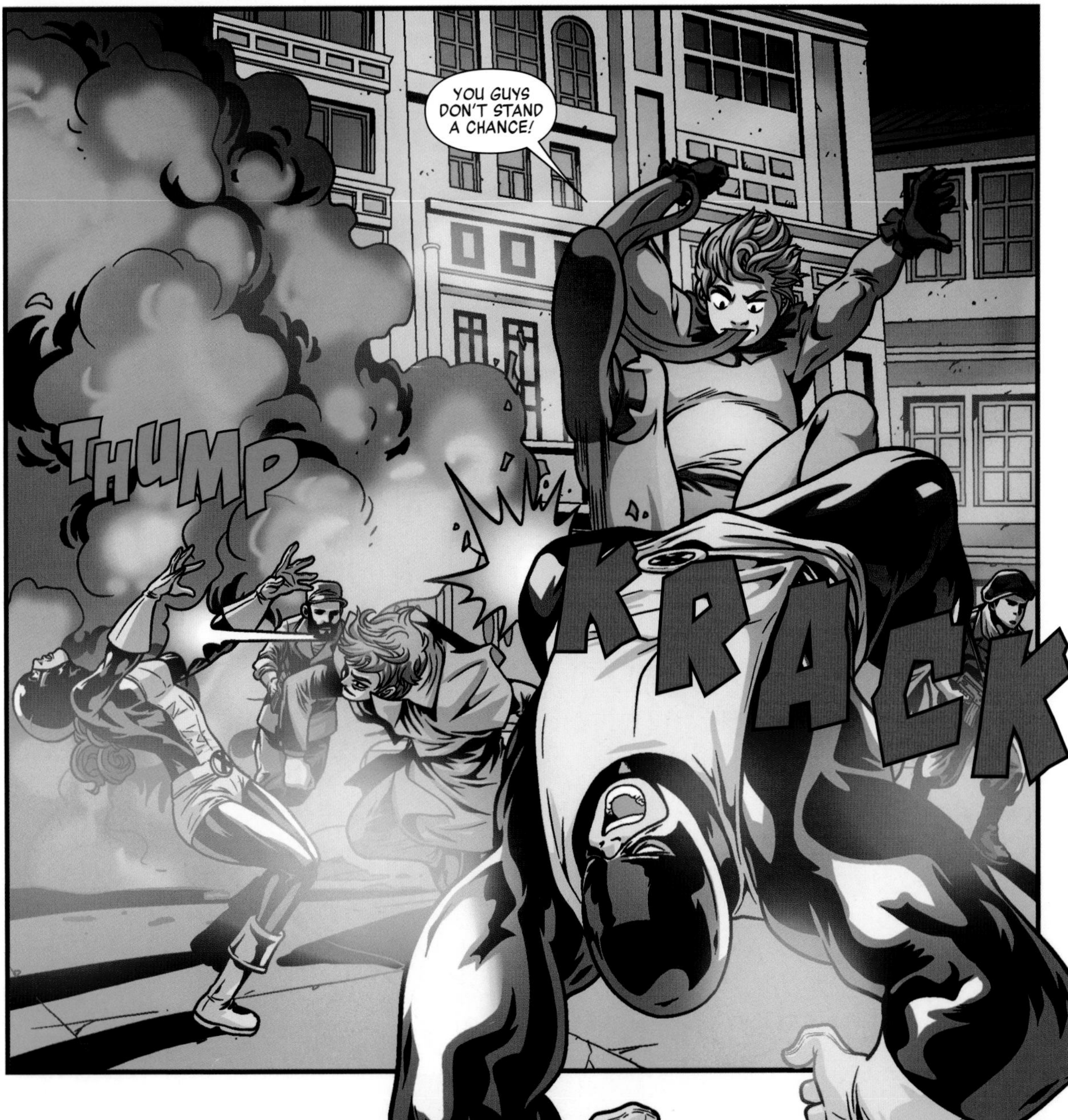
YOU GUYS DON'T STAND A CHANCE!
THUMP
KRACK

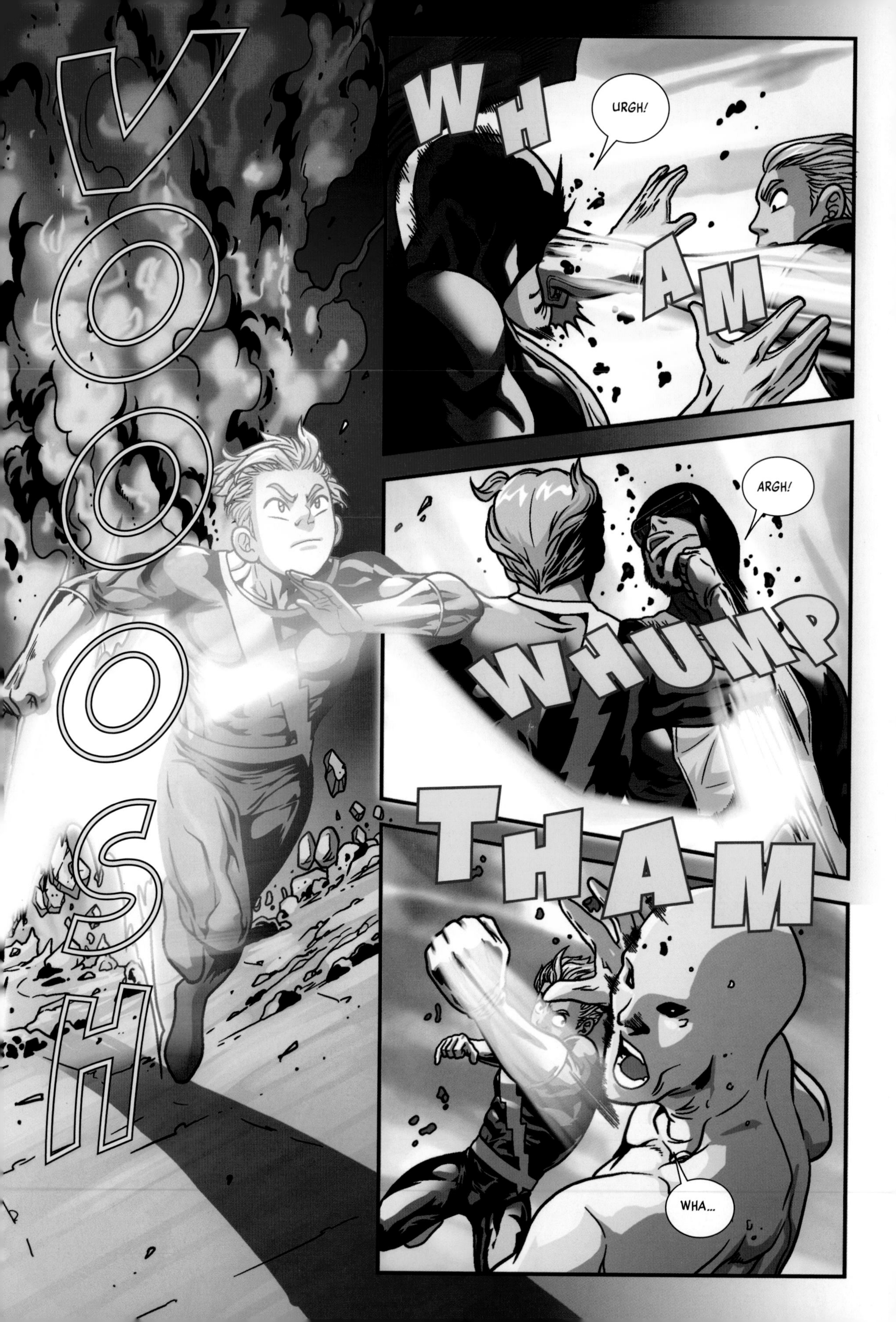
VOOOOSH
WH
URGH!
AM
ARGH!
WHUMP
THAM
WHA...

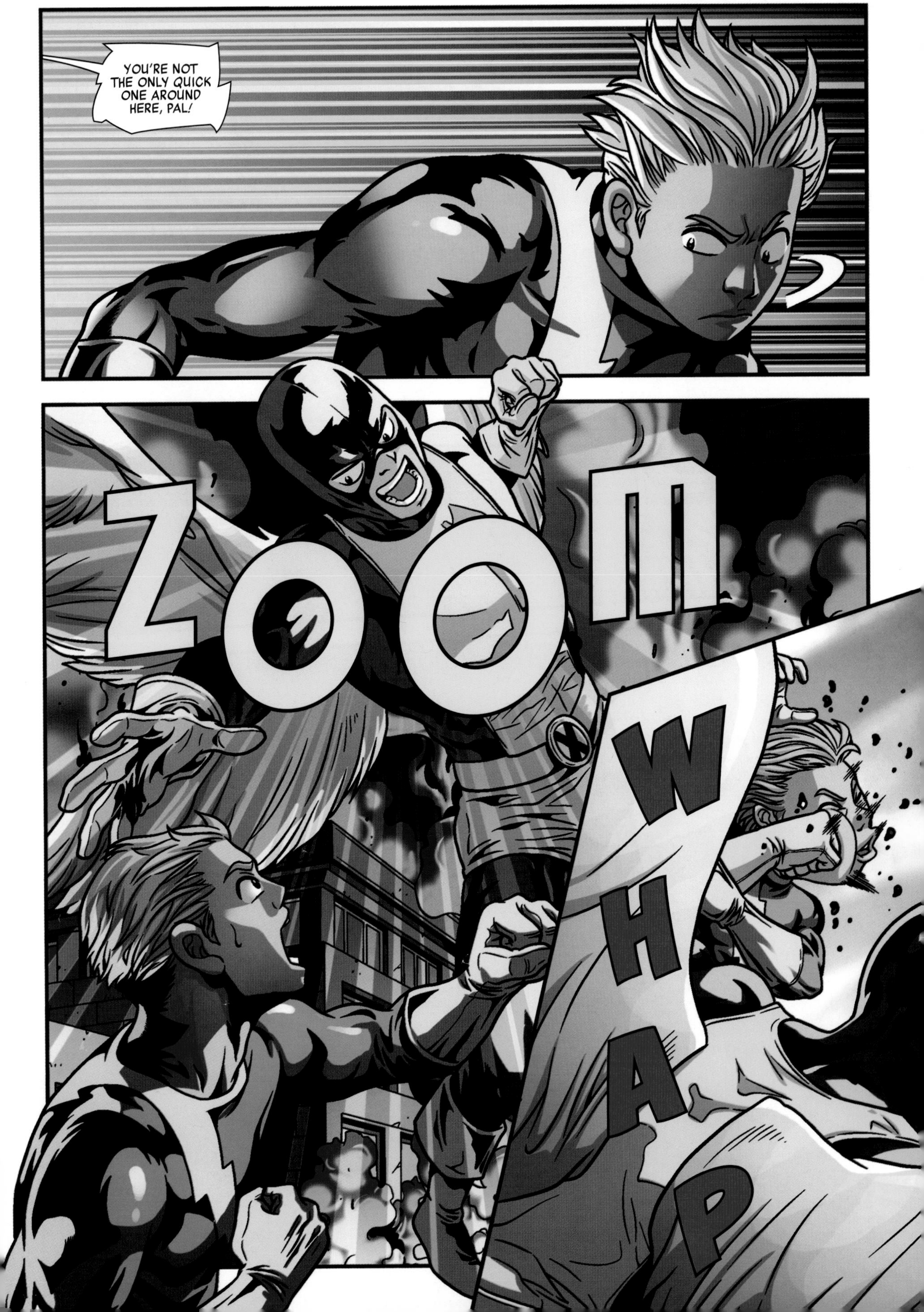
YOU'RE NOT THE ONLY QUICK ONE AROUND HERE, PAL!
ZOOM
WHAP

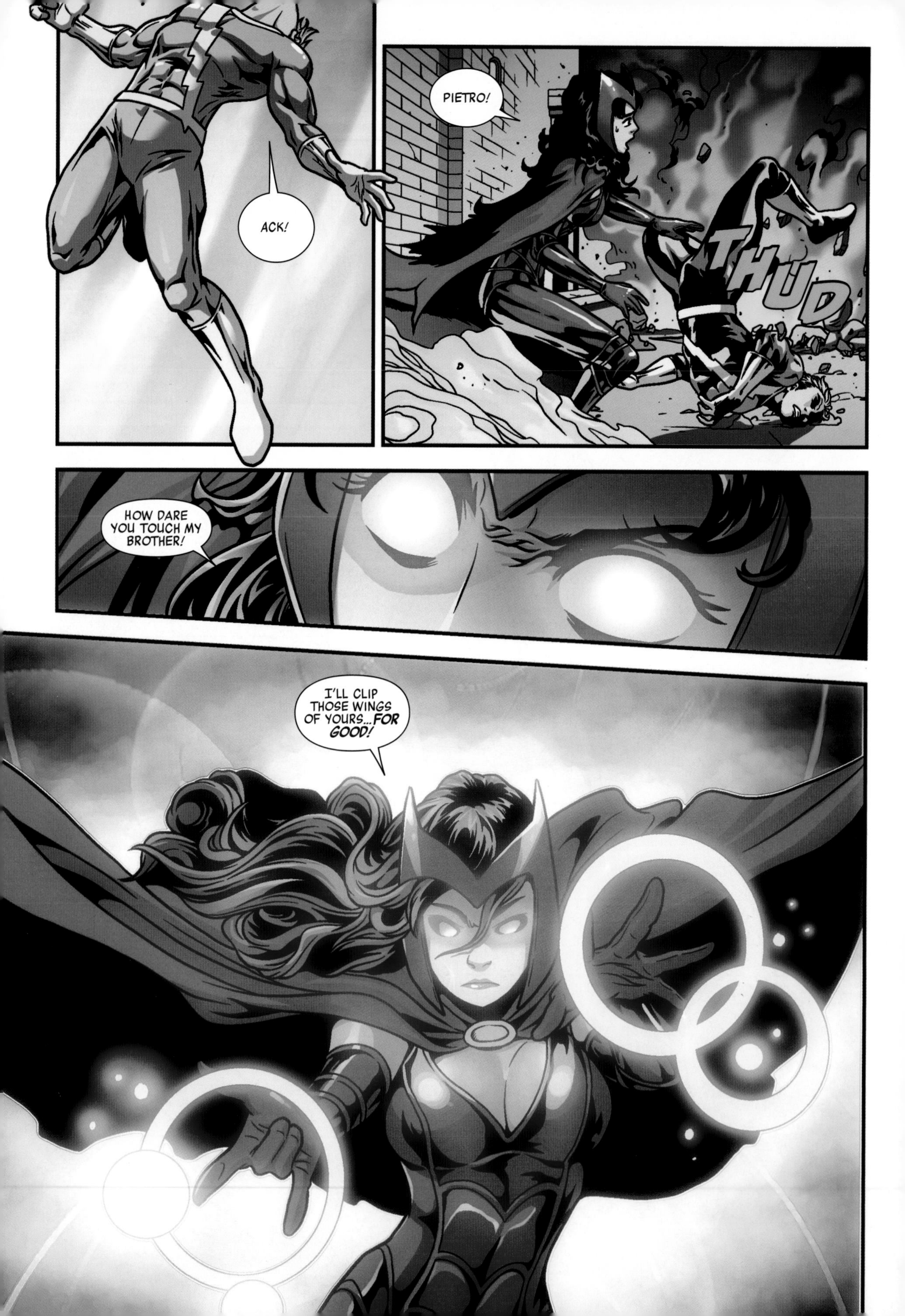
ACK!
PIETRO!
THUD
HOW DARE YOU TOUCH MY BROTHER!
I'LL CLIP THOSE WINGS OF YOURS... **FOR GOOD!**

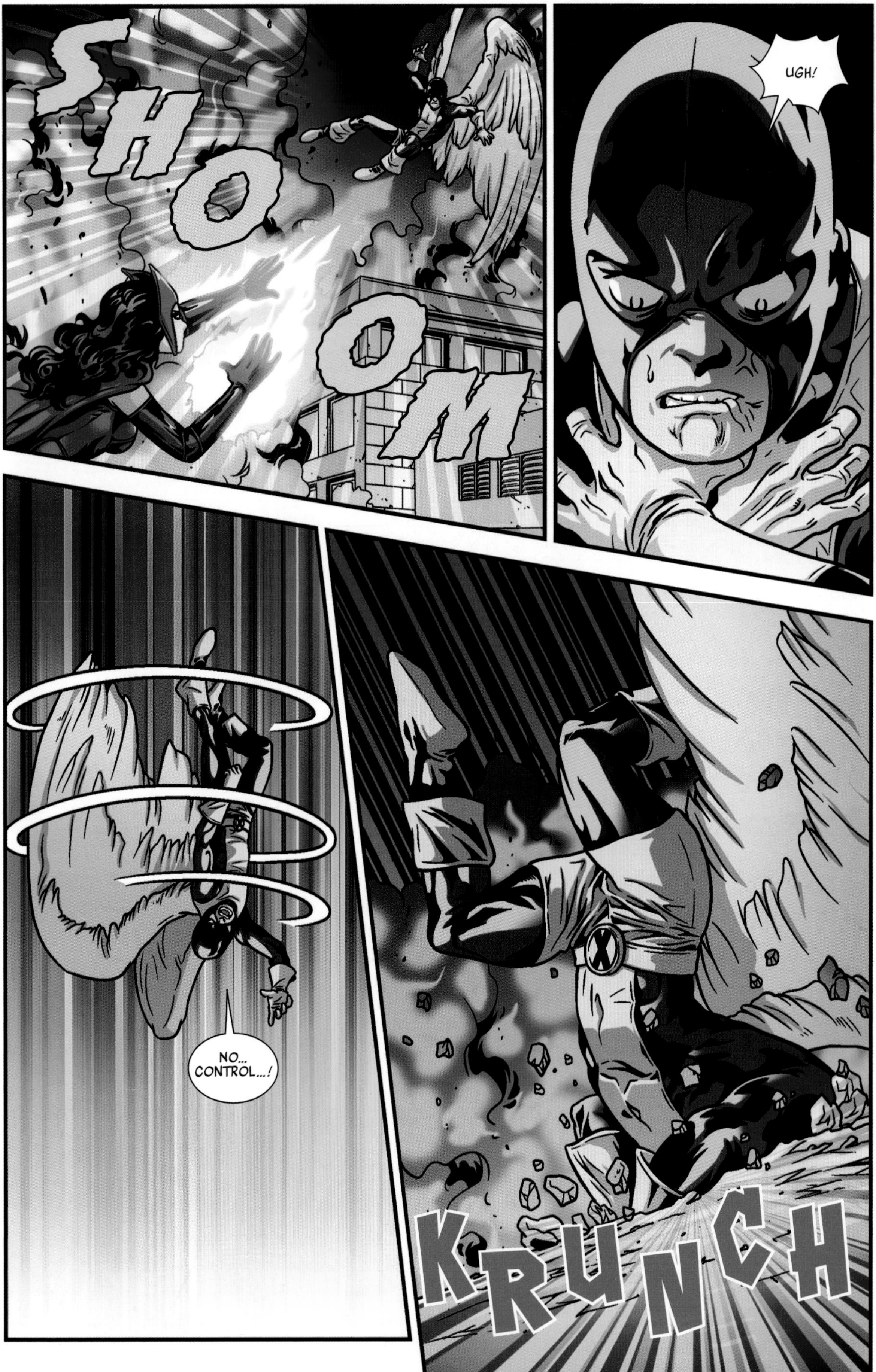
SHOOOM
UGH!
NO... CONTROL...!
KRUNCH

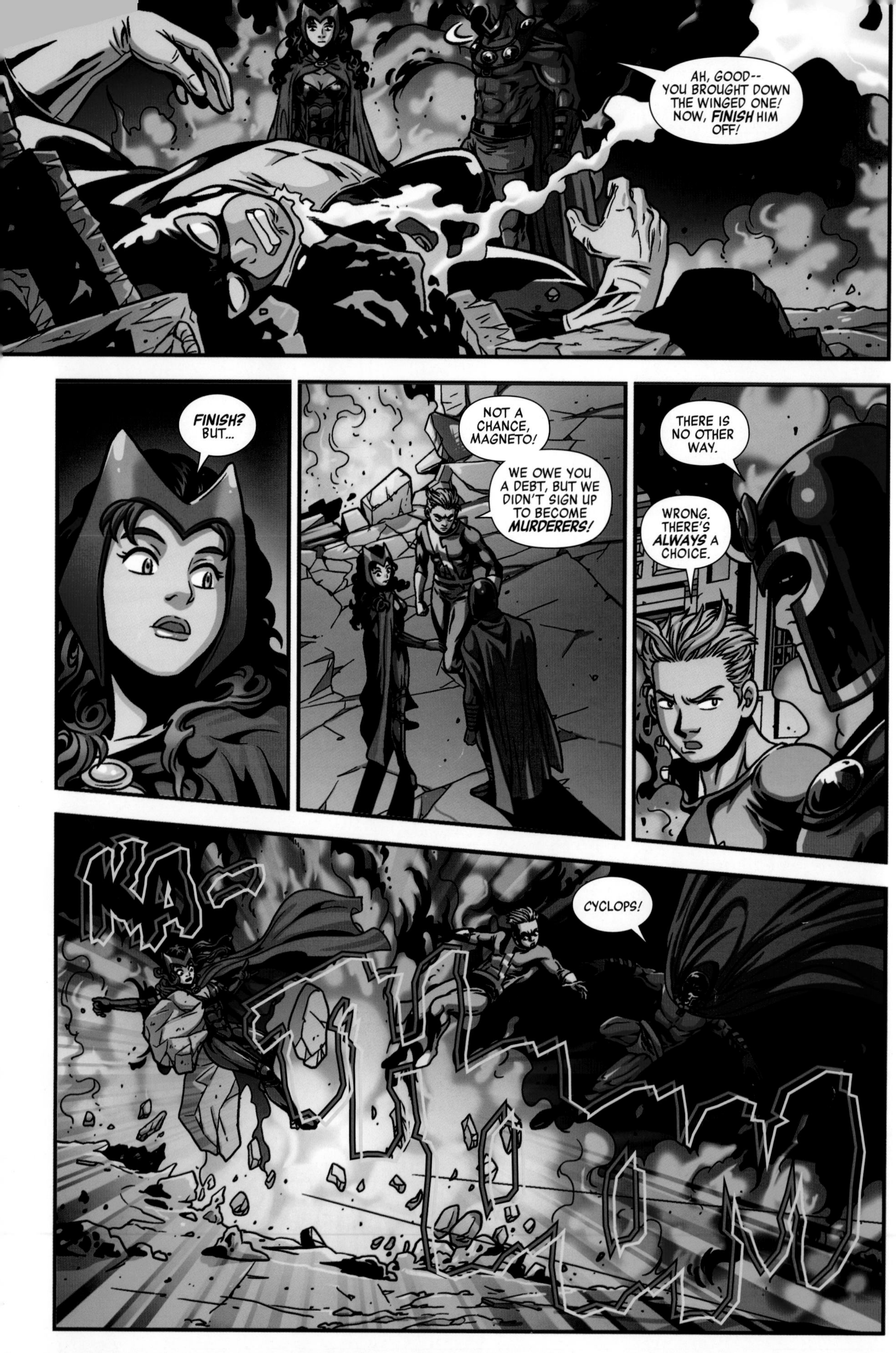
AH, GOOD-- YOU BROUGHT DOWN THE WINGED ONE! NOW, FINISH HIM OFF!
FINISH? BUT...
NOT A CHANCE, MAGNETO!
WE OWE YOU A DEBT, BUT WE DIDN'T SIGN UP TO BECOME MURDERERS!
THERE IS NO OTHER WAY.
WRONG. THERE'S ALWAYS A CHOICE.
KA-
CYCLOPS!

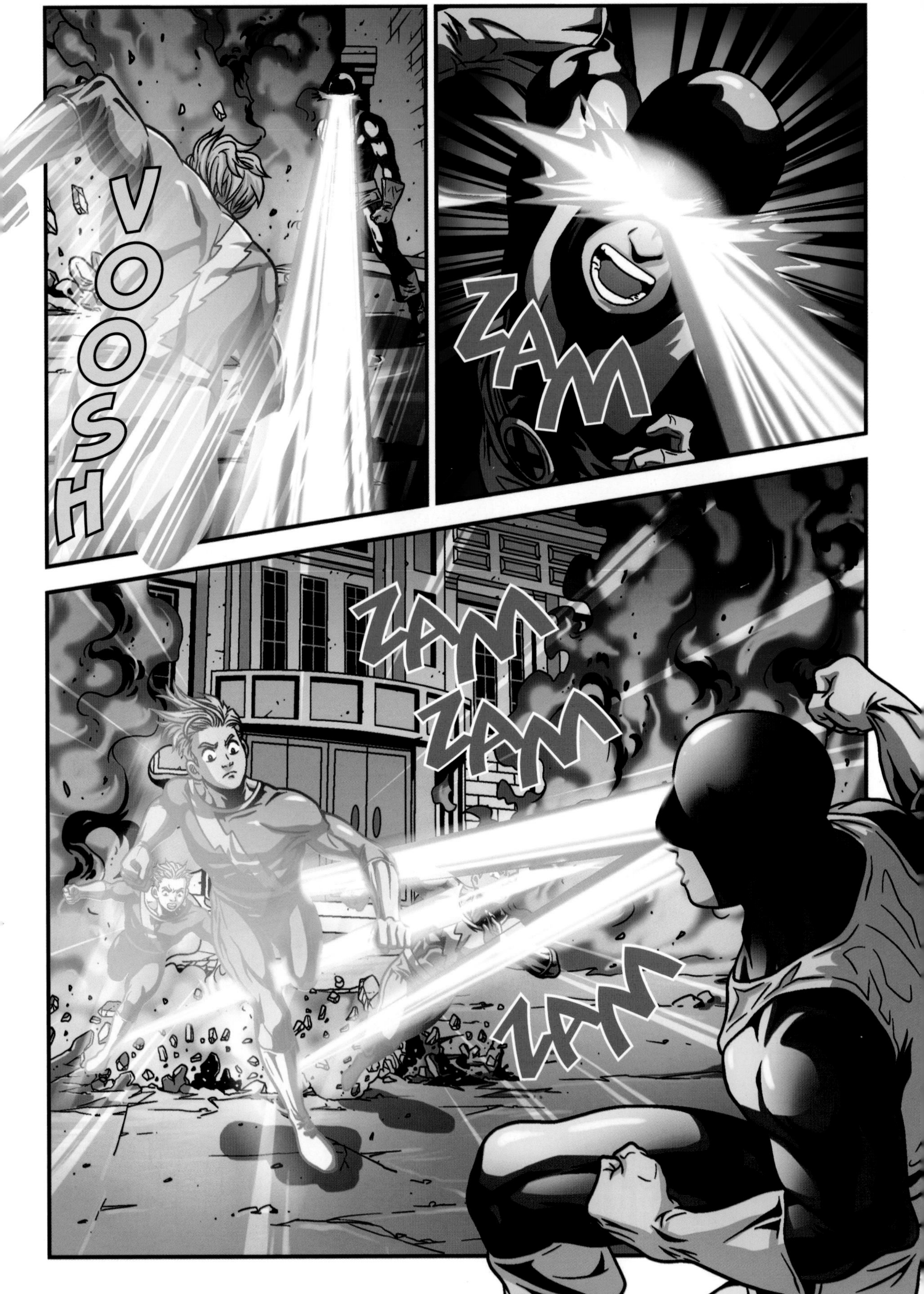
VOOSH
ZAM
ZAM
ZAM
ZAM

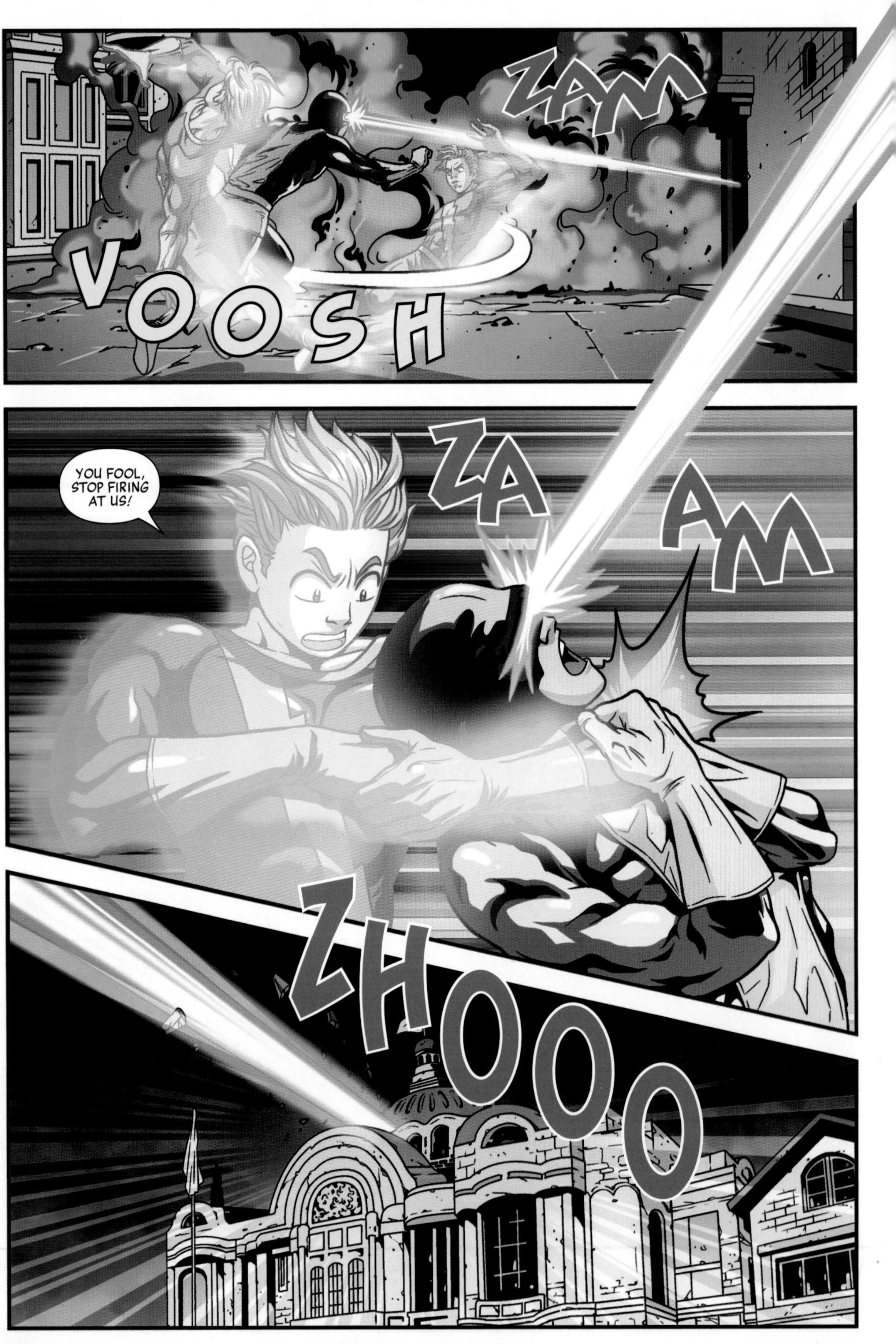
ZAM
VOOSH
YOU FOOL, STOP FIRING AT US!
ZA AM
ZHOOOO

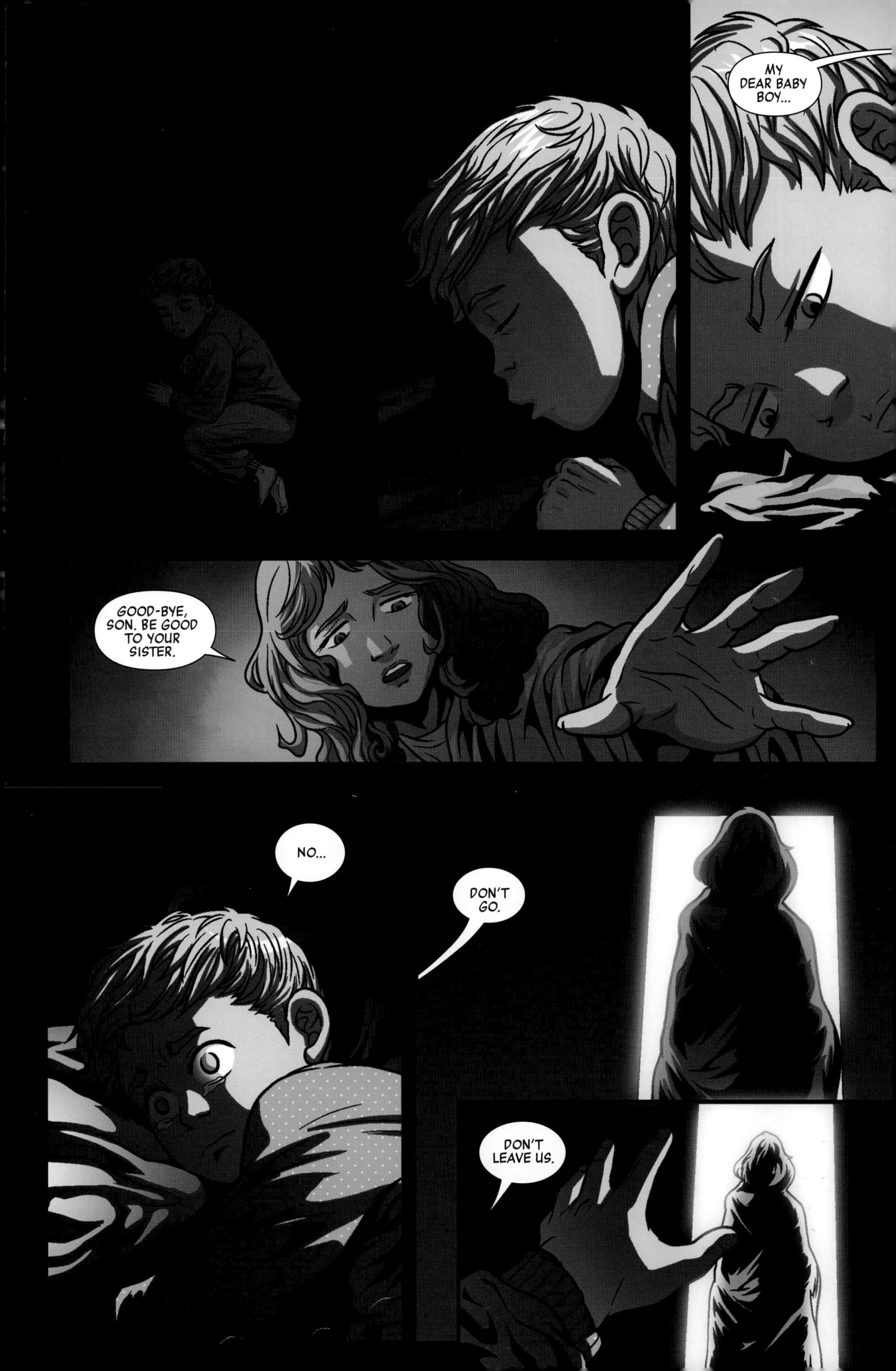
MY DEAR BABY BOY...
GOOD-BYE, SON. BE GOOD TO YOUR SISTER.
NO...
DON'T GO.
DON'T LEAVE US.

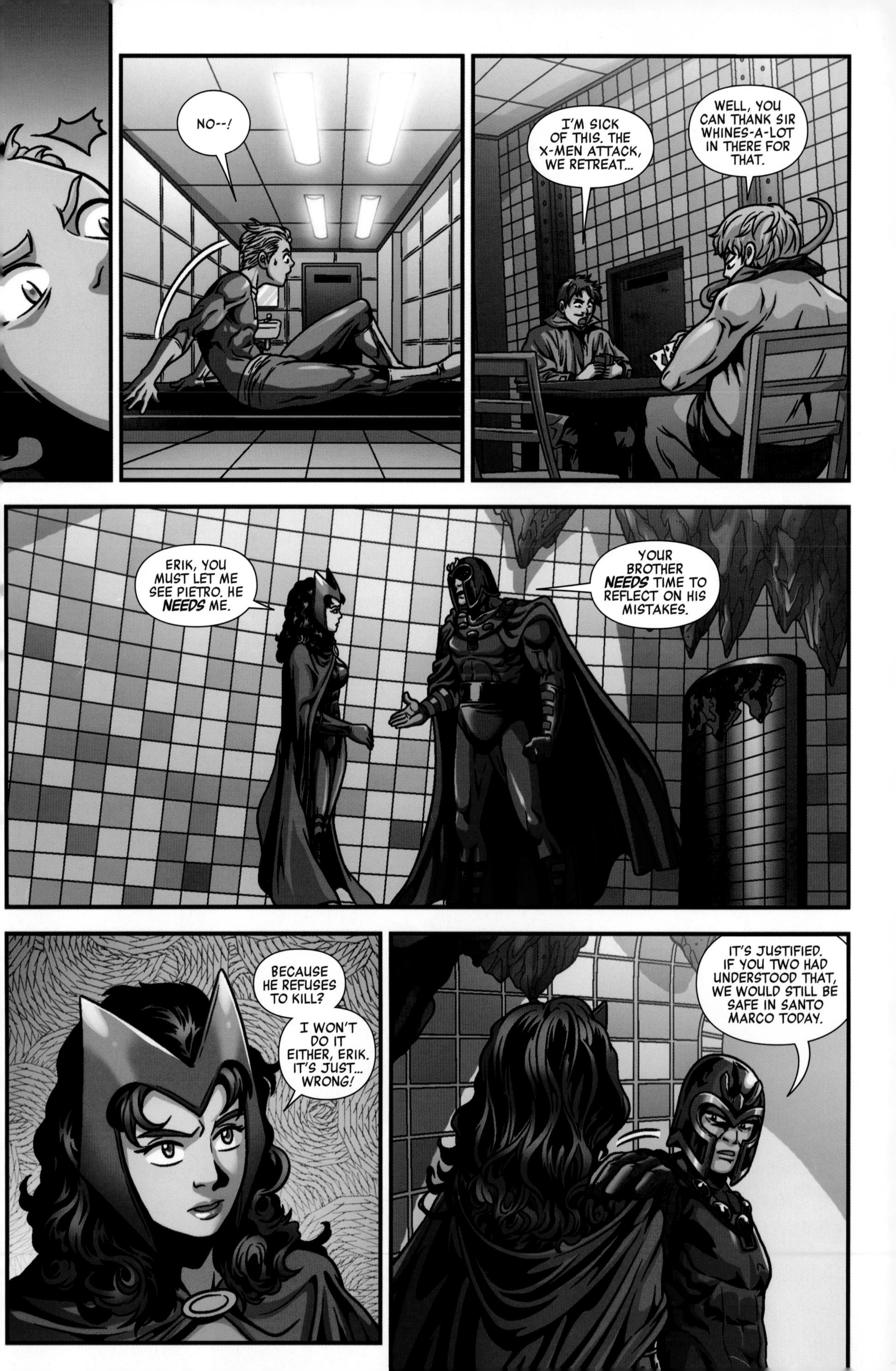
NO--!
I'M SICK OF THIS. THE X-MEN ATTACK, WE RETREAT...
WELL, YOU CAN THANK SIR WHINES-A-LOT IN THERE FOR THAT.
ERIK, YOU MUST LET ME SEE PIETRO. HE NEEDS ME.
YOUR BROTHER NEEDS TIME TO REFLECT ON HIS MISTAKES.
BECAUSE HE REFUSES TO KILL?
I WON'T DO IT EITHER, ERIK. IT'S JUST... WRONG!
IT'S JUSTIFIED. IF YOU TWO HAD UNDERSTOOD THAT, WE WOULD STILL BE SAFE IN SANTO MARCO TODAY.

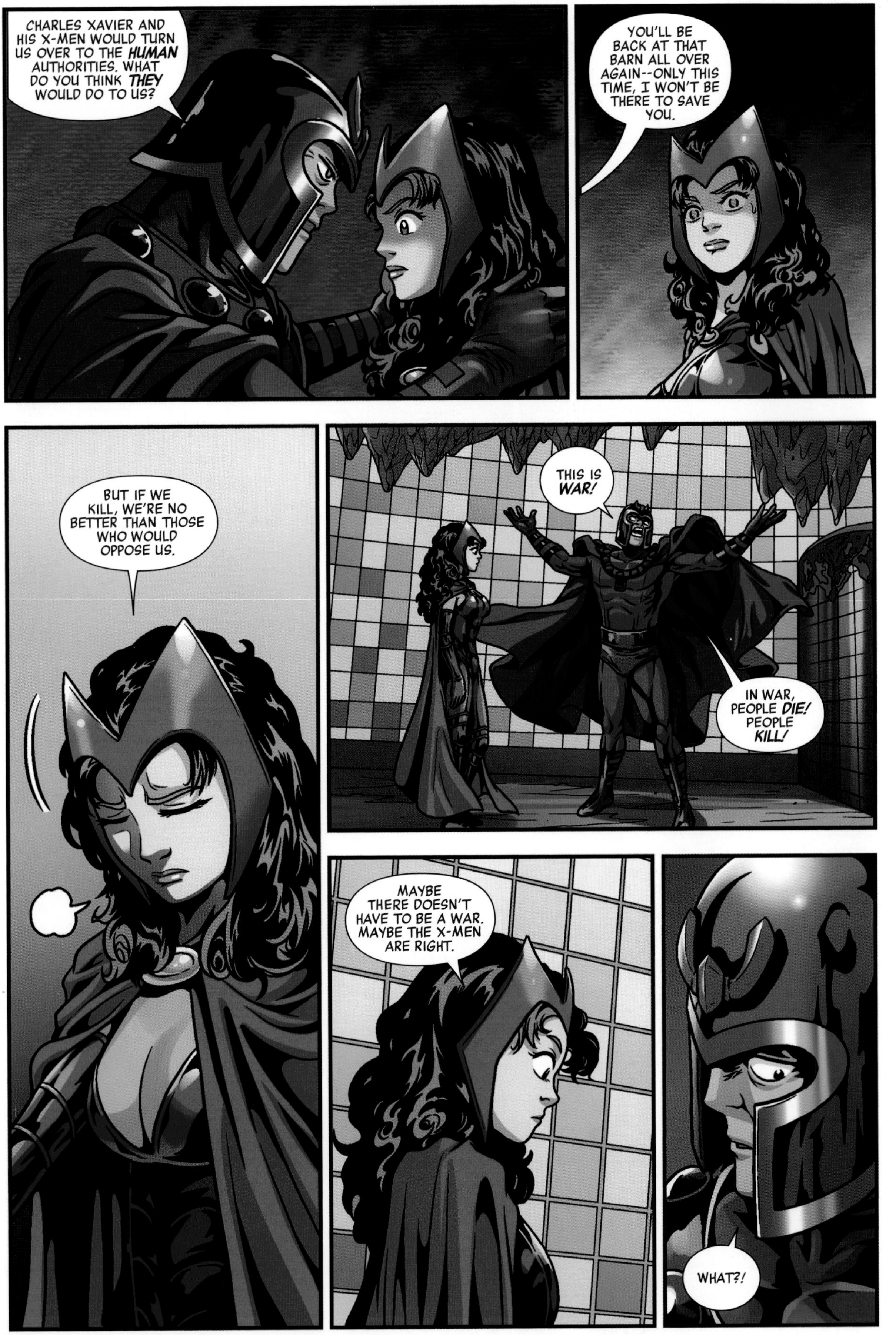
CHARLES XAVIER AND HIS X-MEN WOULD TURN US OVER TO THE HUMAN AUTHORITIES. WHAT DO YOU THINK THEY WOULD DO TO US?
YOU'LL BE BACK AT THAT BARN ALL OVER AGAIN--ONLY THIS TIME, I WON'T BE THERE TO SAVE YOU.
BUT IF WE KILL, WE'RE NO BETTER THAN THOSE WHO WOULD OPPOSE US.
THIS IS WAR!
IN WAR, PEOPLE DIE! PEOPLE KILL!
MAYBE THERE DOESN'T HAVE TO BE A WAR. MAYBE THE X-MEN ARE RIGHT.
WHAT?!

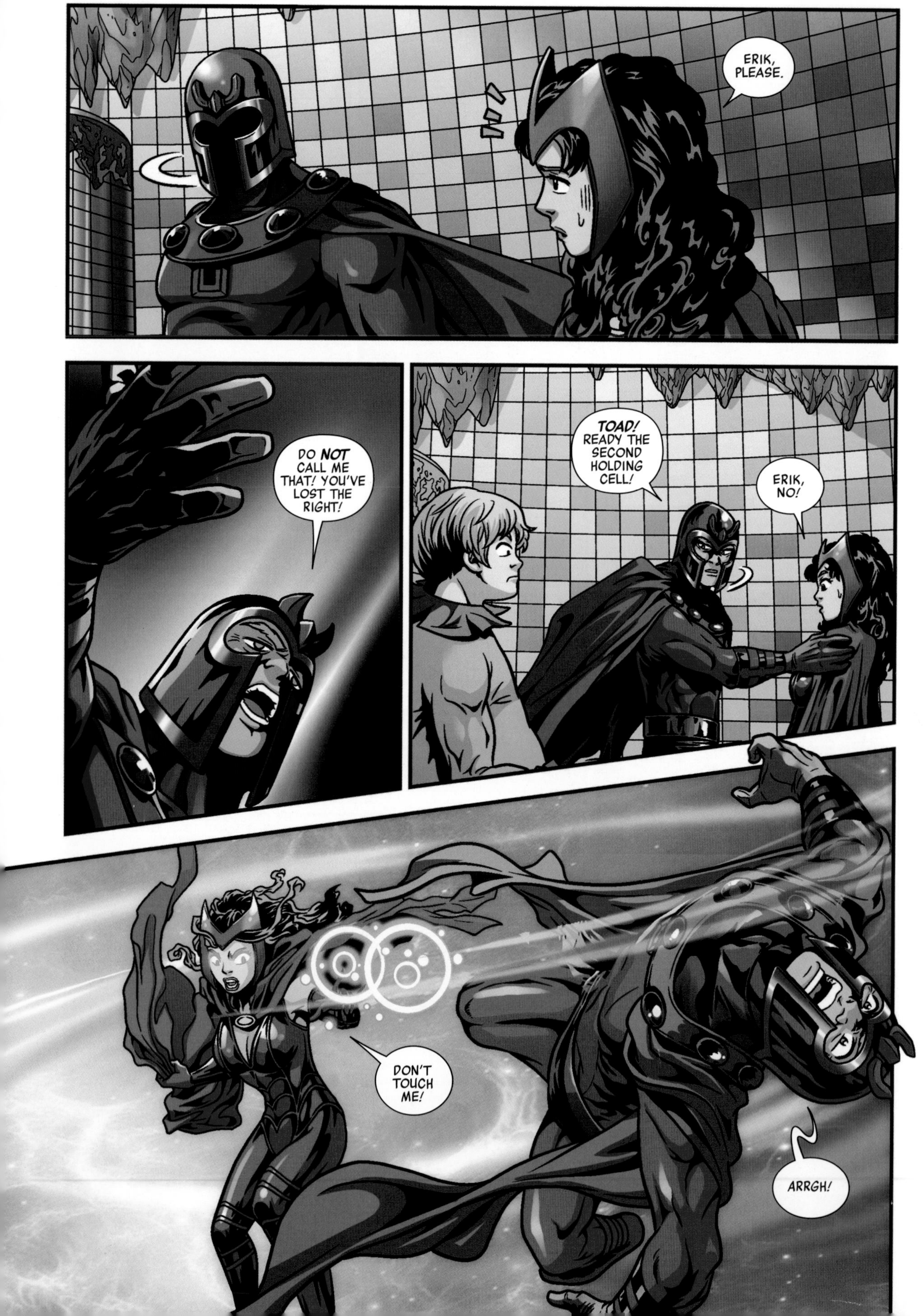
ERIK, PLEASE.
DO **NOT** CALL ME THAT! YOU'VE LOST THE RIGHT!
TOAD! READY THE SECOND HOLDING CELL!
ERIK, NO!
DON'T TOUCH ME!
ARRGH!

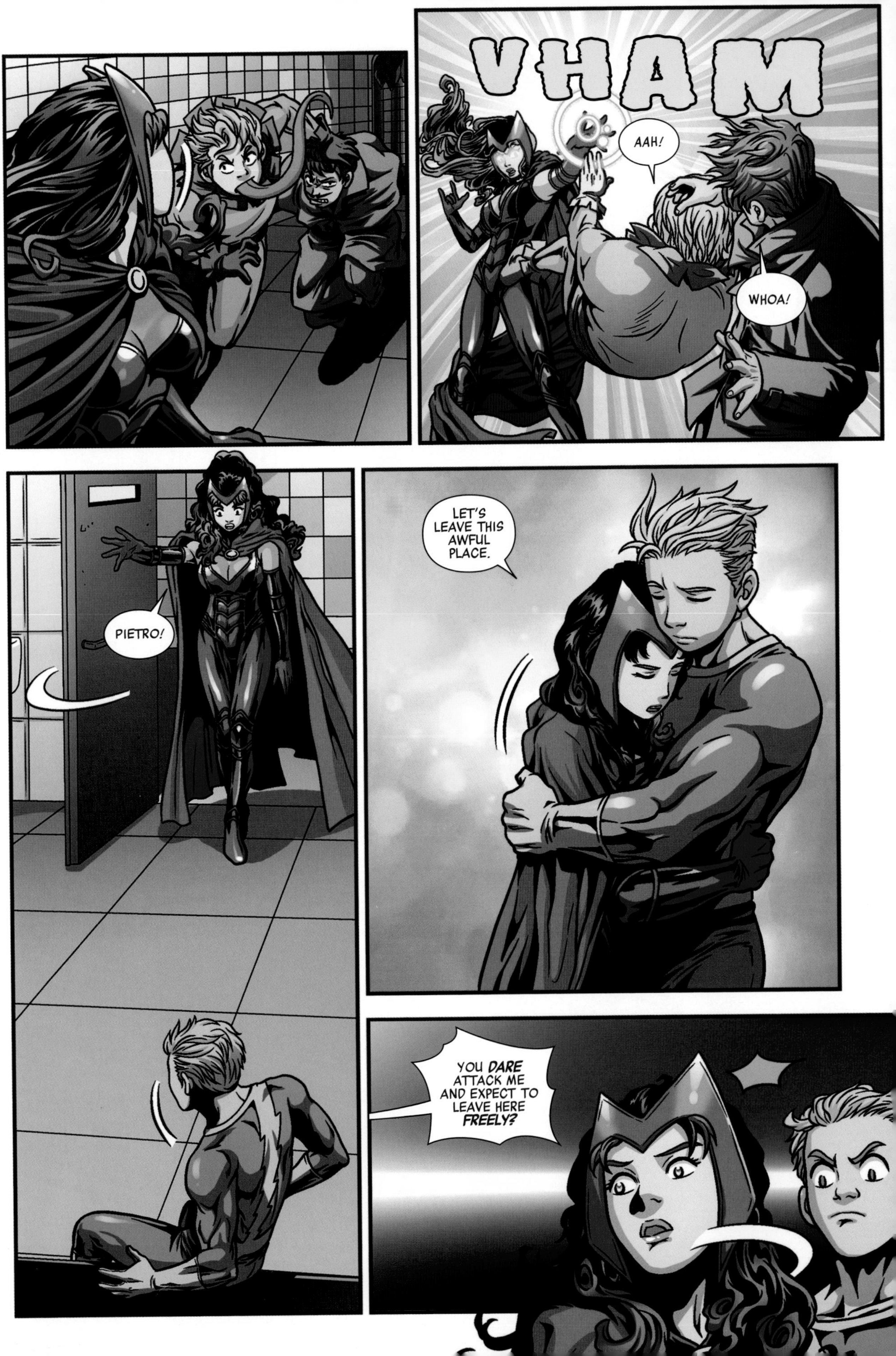
VHAM
AAH!
WHOA!
PIETRO!
LET'S LEAVE THIS AWFUL PLACE.
YOU DARE ATTACK ME AND EXPECT TO LEAVE HERE FREELY?

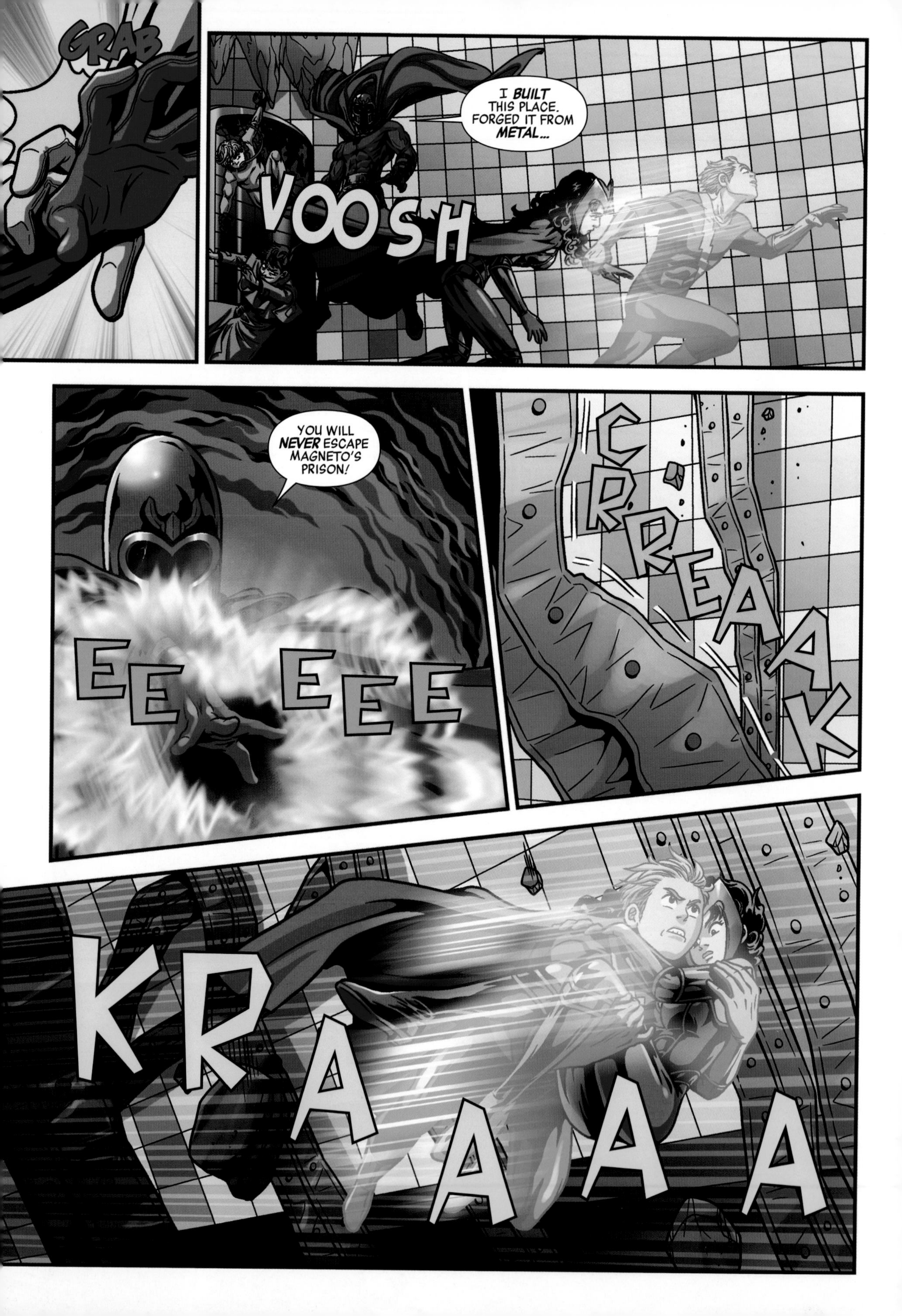

GRAB
I BUILT THIS PLACE. FORGED IT FROM METAL...
VOOSH
YOU WILL NEVER ESCAPE MAGNETO'S PRISON!
EE EEE
CRREAAK
KRAAAA

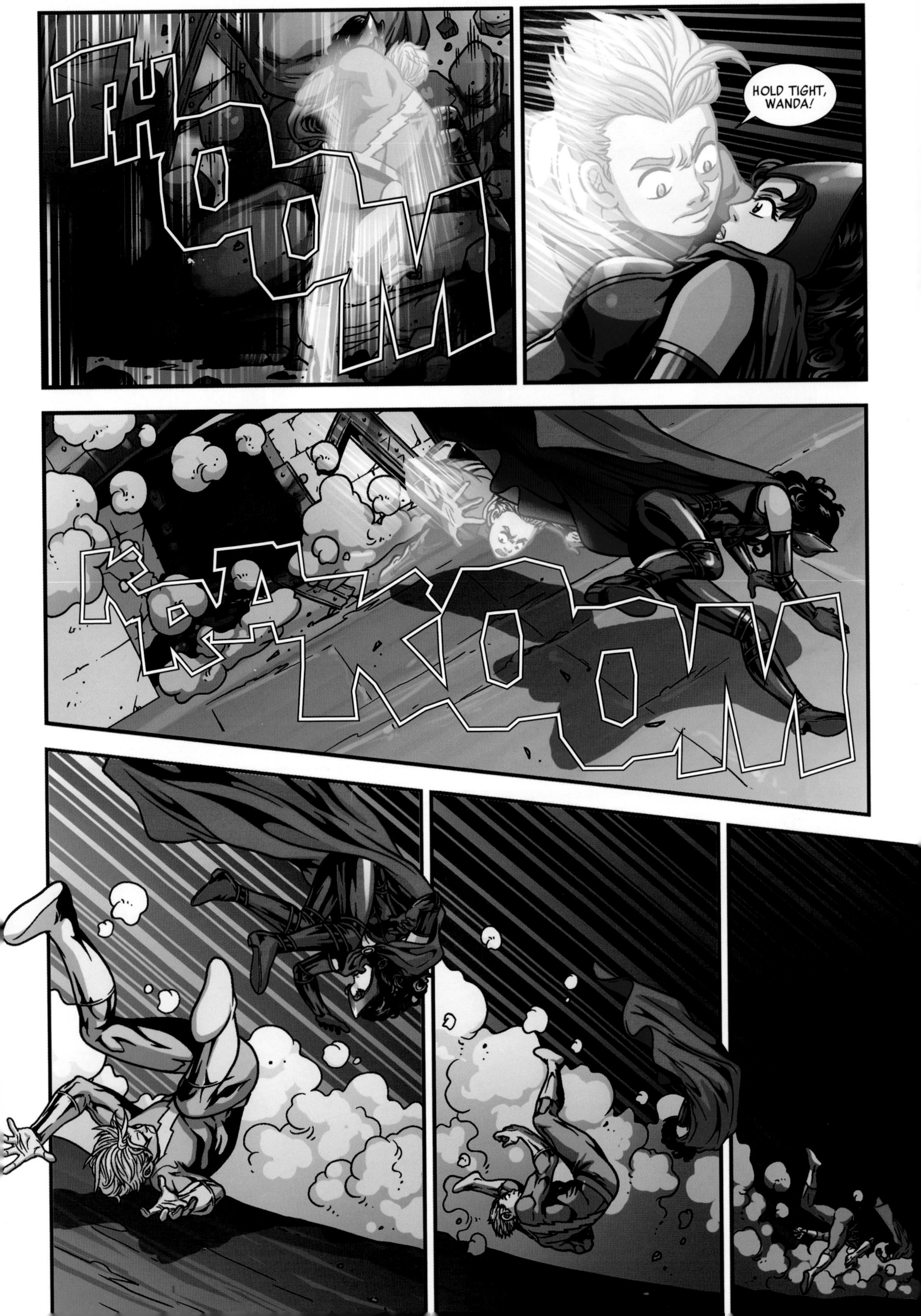
THOOM
HOLD TIGHT, WANDA!
KRAKOOM

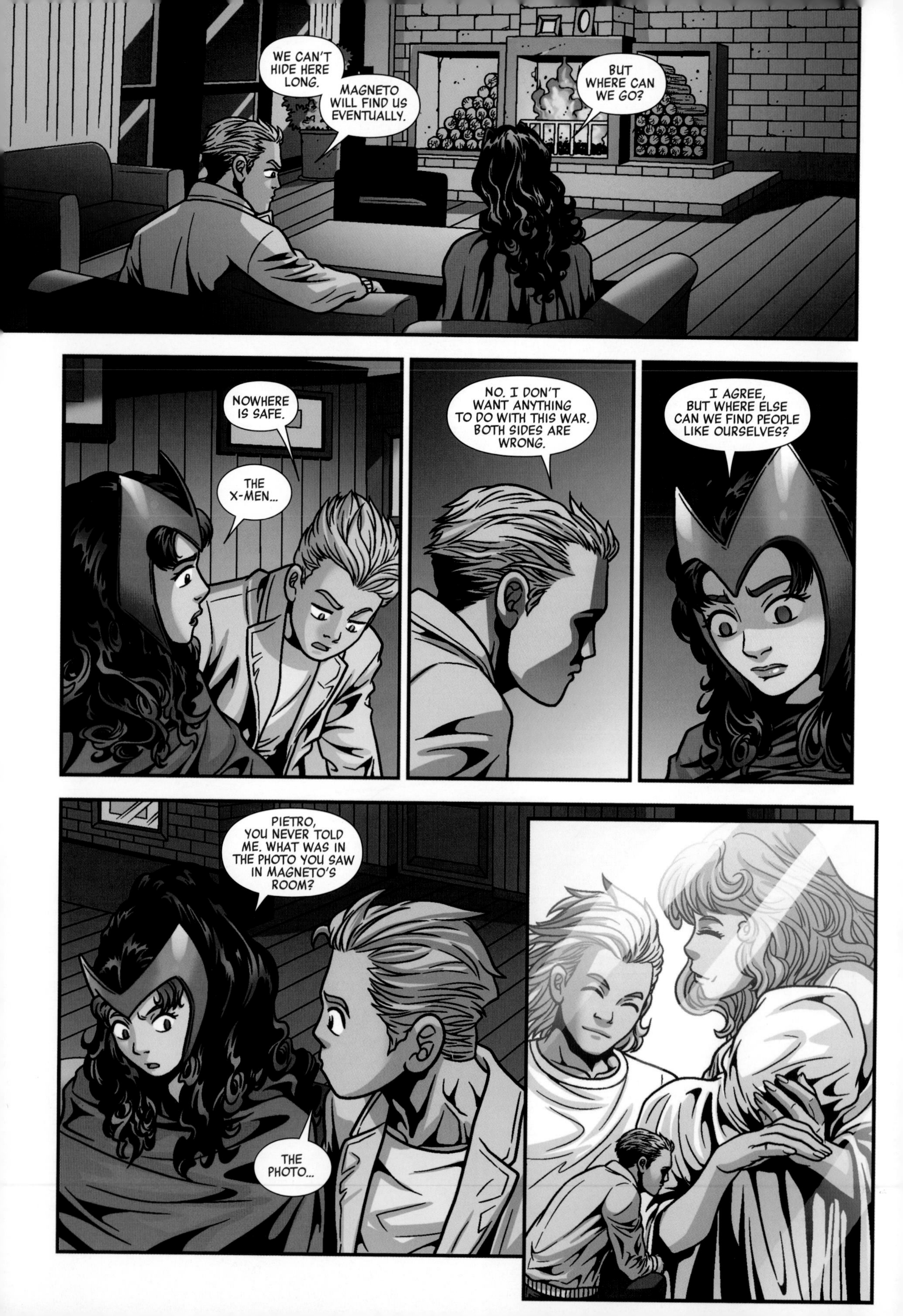

WE CAN'T HIDE HERE LONG.
MAGNETO WILL FIND US EVENTUALLY.
BUT WHERE CAN WE GO?
NOWHERE IS SAFE.
THE X-MEN...
NO. I DON'T WANT ANYTHING TO DO WITH THIS WAR. BOTH SIDES ARE WRONG.
I AGREE, BUT WHERE ELSE CAN WE FIND PEOPLE LIKE OURSELVES?
PIETRO, YOU NEVER TOLD ME. WHAT WAS IN THE PHOTO YOU SAW IN MAGNETO'S ROOM?
THE PHOTO...

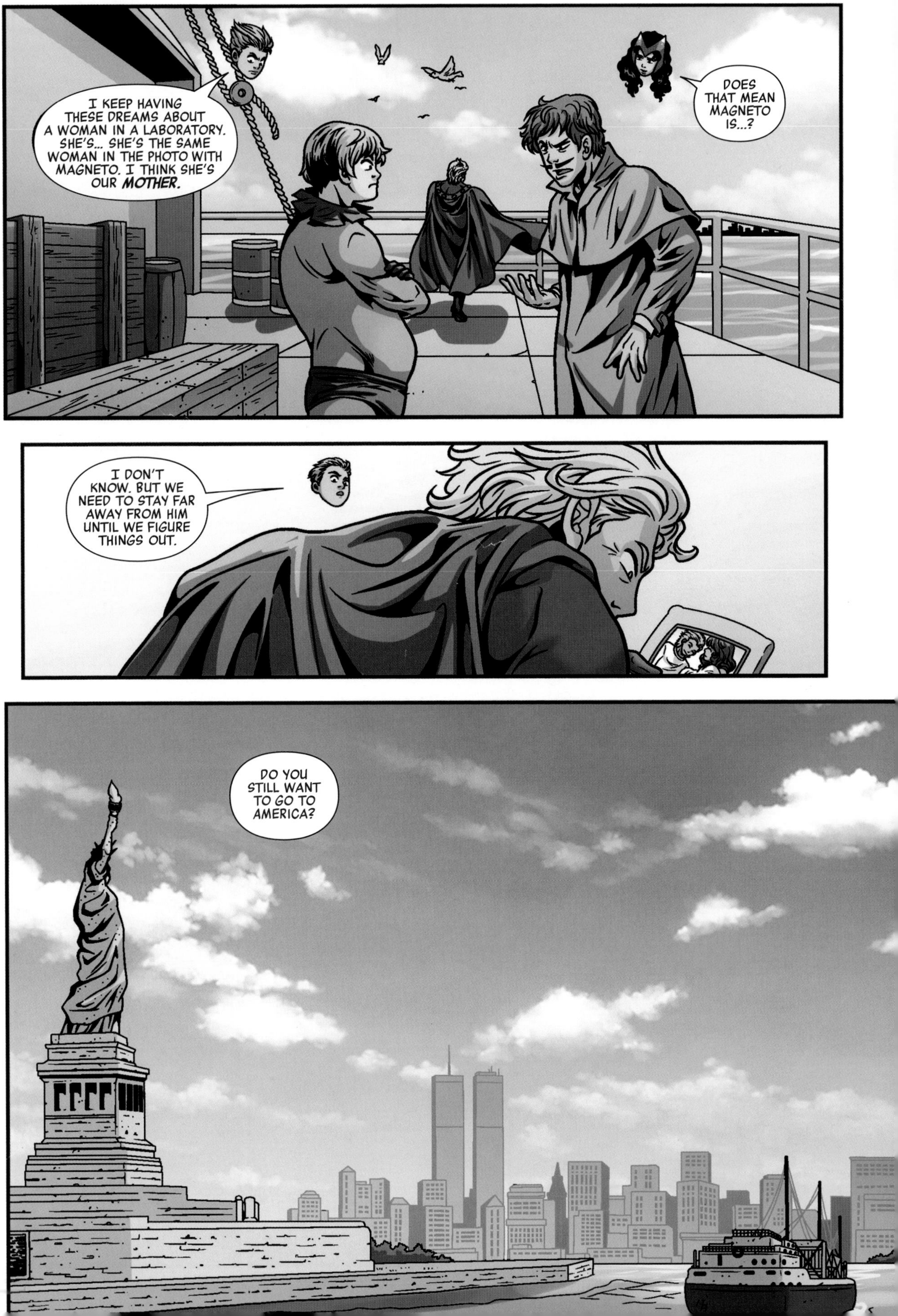
I KEEP HAVING THESE DREAMS ABOUT A WOMAN IN A LABORATORY. SHE'S... SHE'S THE SAME WOMAN IN THE PHOTO WITH MAGNETO. I THINK SHE'S OUR *MOTHER.*
DOES THAT MEAN MAGNETO IS...?
I DON'T KNOW. BUT WE NEED TO STAY FAR AWAY FROM HIM UNTIL WE FIGURE THINGS OUT.
DO YOU STILL WANT TO GO TO AMERICA?

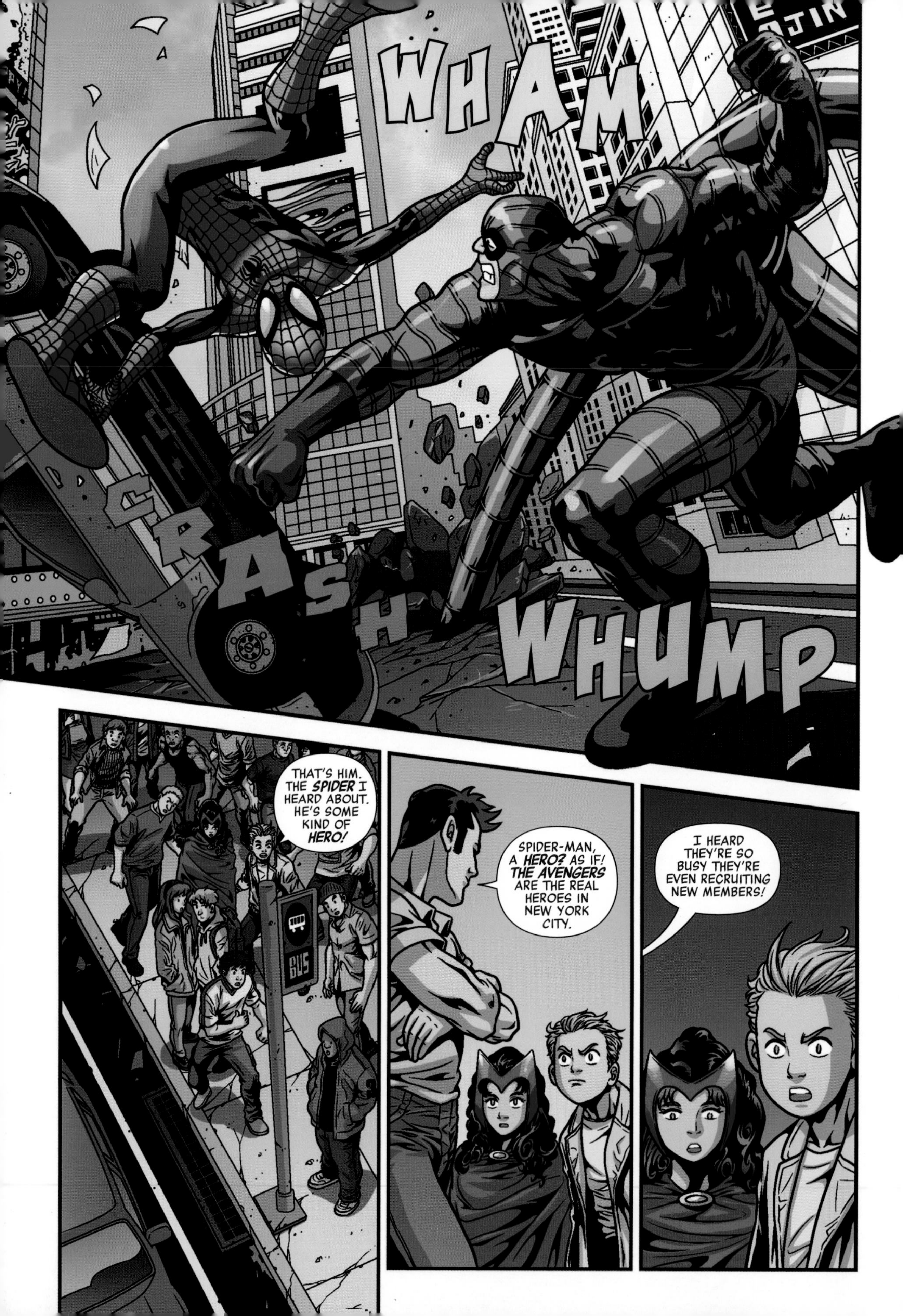

WHAM
CRASH
WHUMP
THAT'S HIM. THE SPIDER I HEARD ABOUT. HE'S SOME KIND OF HERO!
BUS
SPIDER-MAN, A HERO? AS IF! THE AVENGERS ARE THE REAL HEROES IN NEW YORK CITY.
I HEARD THEY'RE SO BUSY THEY'RE EVEN RECRUITING NEW MEMBERS!

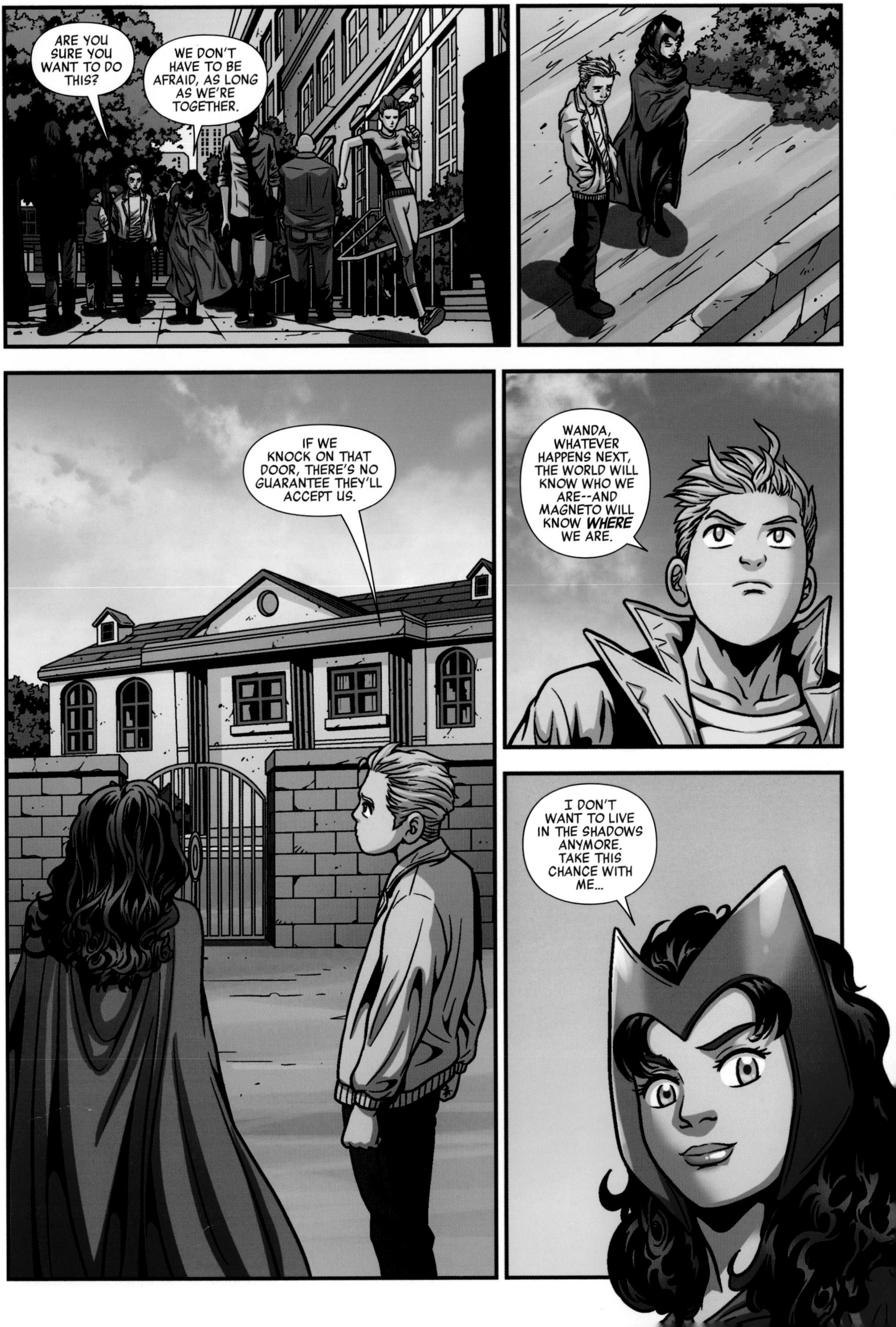
ARE YOU SURE YOU WANT TO DO THIS?
WE DON'T HAVE TO BE AFRAID, AS LONG AS WE'RE TOGETHER.
IF WE KNOCK ON THAT DOOR, THERE'S NO GUARANTEE THEY'LL ACCEPT US.
WANDA, WHATEVER HAPPENS NEXT, THE WORLD WILL KNOW WHO WE ARE--AND MAGNETO WILL KNOW *WHERE* WE ARE.
I DON'T WANT TO LIVE IN THE SHADOWS ANYMORE. TAKE THIS CHANCE WITH ME...

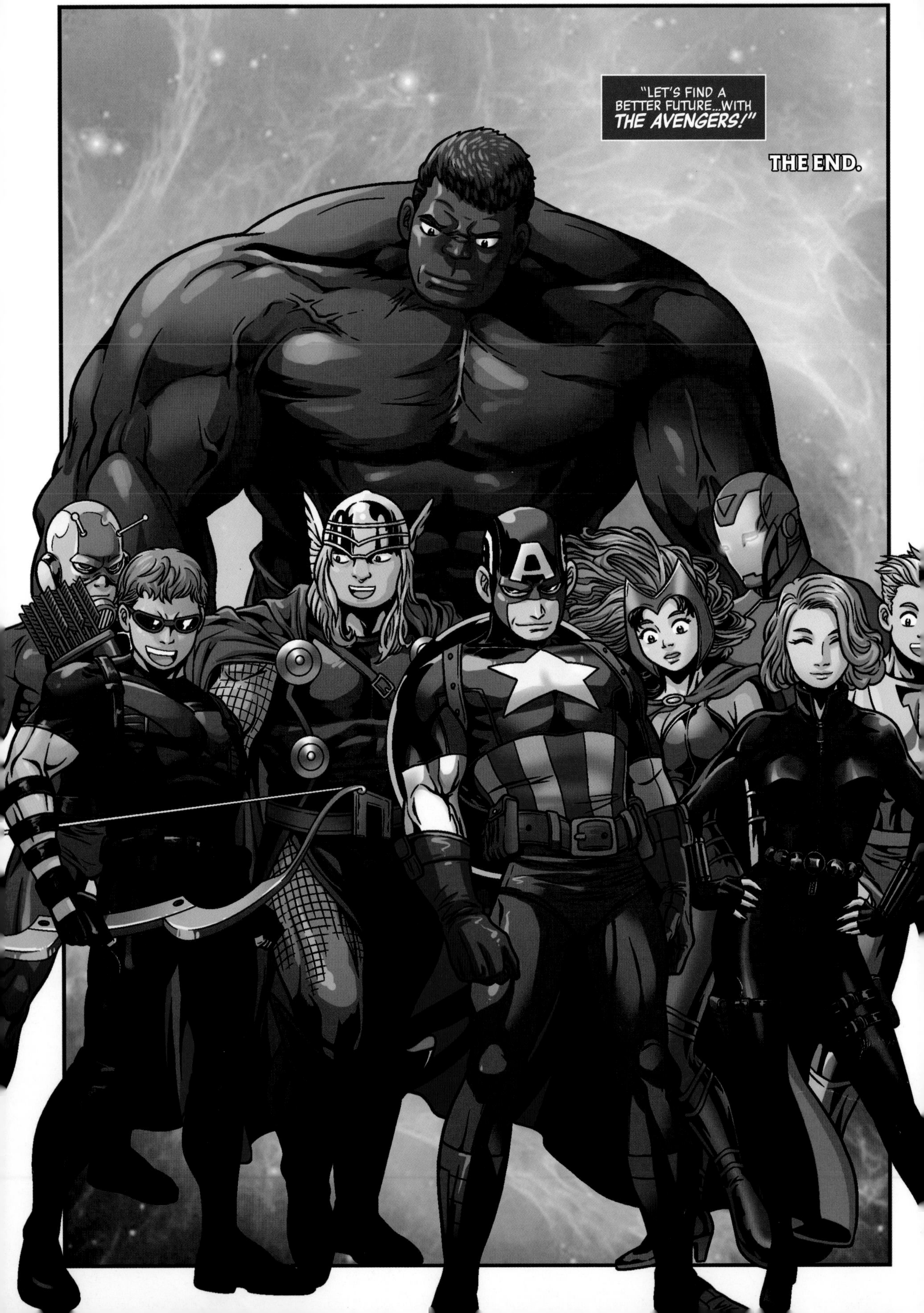
"LET'S FIND A BETTER FUTURE...WITH THE AVENGERS!"
THE END.

AVENGERS K
THE ADVENT OF ULTRON

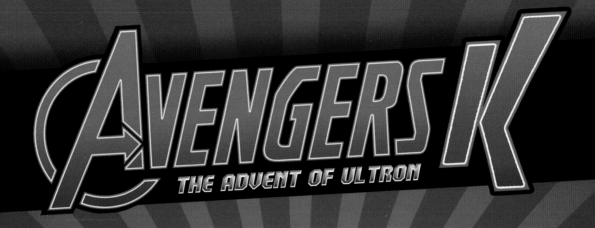

COLLECT THEM ALL!

Set of 6 Hardcover Books ISBN: 978-1-5321-4000-6

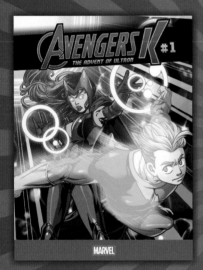

AVENGERS K #1
THE ADVENT OF ULTRON
MARVEL

Hardcover Book ISBN
978-1-5321-4001-3

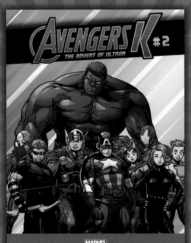

AVENGERS K #2
THE ADVENT OF ULTRON
MARVEL

Hardcover Book ISBN
978-1-5321-4002-0

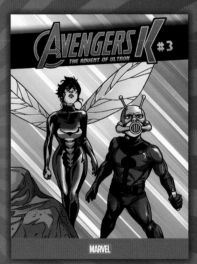

AVENGERS K #3
THE ADVENT OF ULTRON
MARVEL

Hardcover Book ISBN
978-1-5321-4003-7

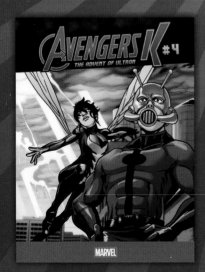

AVENGERS K #4
THE ADVENT OF ULTRON
MARVEL

Hardcover Book ISBN
978-1-5321-4004-4

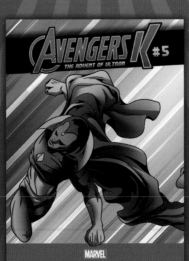

AVENGERS K #5
THE ADVENT OF ULTRON
MARVEL

Hardcover Book ISBN
978-1-5321-4005-1

AVENGERS K #6
THE ADVENT OF ULTRON
MARVEL

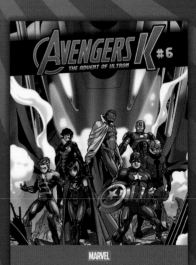

Hardcover Book ISBN
978-1-5321-4006-8